days of courage

Days of Courage

A MEDIEVAL ADVENTURE

Niels Jensen

Translated from the Danish
by Oliver Stallybrass

Published in England under the title
When the Land Lay Waste

Harcourt Brace Jovanovich, Inc.
New York

Originally published in Denmark
by Gyldendal in 1971 under the title of *Da landet lå øde*

First American edition, 1973
Printed in the United States of America
B C D E F G H I J K

Library of Congress Cataloging in Publication Data

Jensen, Niels.
Days of courage: a medieval adventure.

SUMMARY: A boy and a girl in medieval Denmark journey through a land ravaged by the plague in search of a surviving relative.

[1. Black death—Fiction. 2. Denmark—Fiction]
I. Title.

PZ7.J435Day [Fic] 73-5241
ISBN 0-15-222880-2

days of courage

CHAPTER 1

The yellow mud-built houses lay wrapped in silence. There was no lowing of cows, no grunting of pigs. And no dogs—dogs that normally kick up a fearful uproar when strangers come to a village. No women's voices either—women, who are perpetually bawling to each other from door to door across the village street about the little one's gripes, about the sow and her nine piebald piglets, about the hundred-and-one things that women chatter and bawl about.

From his vantage point he could see that every door stood open, human doors, cow doors, horse doors—the lot! He could peer along the crests of many of the gray thatched roofs. But nowhere was there any sign of life—not a single column of smoke from a single smoke hole.

The entire village was so silent that it must be deserted. A number of the bulging mud walls were daubed with great black crosses, such as he had seen in many other places—three black tarred crosses in a row.

The stone wall of the churchyard commanded a

good view of the village. That was why he had scrambled up onto the granite boulders.

There he stood, a thin, scraggy boy with reddish hair that was long and matted. His face looked too small under all that hair, and the little that showed was grimy in the extreme—all gray and white streaks and big black marks. It was the sort of face you get from rubbing your eyes with hands covered in earth—and from crying.

A flock of great black birds flew up from a farm at the other end of the village. The boy on the wall started at the sudden flapping noise and the strange, hoarse cries, almost like the barking of dogs. He stood openmouthed, watching their approach and shielding his eyes from the glare of the sun, which was about to disappear behind the trees on the common.

Some of the birds flew directly over his head, then settled on the roof ridge of the thatched church. Others continued over the fields in an easterly direction; for a long time he could still hear their hoarse barking—while his eyes remained on the roof of the church. The black ravens were sitting there watching him. Hungrily, he thought. One of them settled on the bell tower by the west gable.

In many parts of the churchyard the grass needed cutting, and weeds were growing luxuriantly: milfoil, ground elder, and enormous green ferns. Between the scattered juniper bushes there were small gray mounds of earth in large numbers, and all the same size. He tried to count them, but by the time he reached the farthest ones, right over by the wall of the church, he could no longer remember whether it was forty-five or fifty-five.

He turned away quickly and jumped down into the

grass outside the stone wall, pitching forward onto his knees, for it was a big drop; the wall here was higher than the one back home at Ullsthorp. He picked himself up and began making his way between the houses in the village street.

On his back was a leather bag, securely fastened with a strap so as to leave both hands free. The bag lay across his shoulders, making him look like a hunchback; this he could see from his shadow. The sleeves of his gray jacket were too short, and his knee breeches were frayed at the edges, as happens from constant brushing against the bushes and undergrowth.

He picked his way carefully between the houses. He was barefoot and there might be things he could cut himself on. At one point he stopped and stood quite still. It was just outside a gateway. He couldn't see anything inside because it was in semidarkness, but he could hear a rattling and a rustling—maybe just rats. In the villages he had seen countless rats, so many that he sometimes dreamed the whole world was full of rats.

Now his face lit up in a great smile. He stood there, all by himself, laughing at the sight of a little speckled hen that emerged clucking from the gateway with a clutch of little yellow chicks following behind. Where had she managed to hide from the rats, he wondered, suddenly overjoyed at her presence. But when the hen saw him, she called with a slightly higher-pitched cluck to her brood, and they disappeared hurriedly around a corner.

"Cluck-cluck-cluck," went the boy, in imitation of the hen. It was extraordinary to hear his own voice in the silent village.

The little hen had gone into the yard of the next farm; he could see her through the gateway in the building facing him. She made straight for the dunghill, which still smelled as dunghills do, although it was rapidly turning green with weeds.

Suddenly a large cock came rushing up. The boy could make out that it was pecking violently at something or other, flapping its wings as it did so and making noises that were more like growls than clucks. At last it straightened up and stood still. Then it gave one more violent peck, and the boy saw that it had pecked a rat to death. The cock craned its neck, flapped its wings, crowed once or twice, and strutted importantly around on its green dunghill as if it owned the whole village.

Should he try to catch it? No, it was too much trouble, and he would need to light a fire. Perhaps he might find something that would be easier to catch. Still, it was a very long time since he had tasted roast capon—not since Christmas. Yes, and now it was summer, and everything was different. So far he had managed with what he had picked up on the way. But now all he had left was a bit of meal at the bottom of his bag. He was going to need some food very shortly.

He continued along the green village street. Here the grass and weeds were growing particularly high. They must have been well manured. He stopped at one of the houses. The door of this one stood open like all the others, and it was so low that he had to bend to go in, although he was not yet fully grown. He stepped carefully over the broad plank that formed the threshold. Once inside, he stood still. It was murky and evil-smelling. He wrinkled his nose as he waited for his eyes to get used to the semidarkness.

Very cautiously he advanced to the fireplace under the smoke hole. A little ash and charcoal were still lying on the flat hearthstones. A circle of larger stones projected upward, designed to keep the fire in its proper place. Over the fireplace a kind of earthenware pot was hanging from a leather strap. There was something or other in the pot, but it had grown a long, greenish beard and smelled of mold.

Somewhere above his head there was a rustling. He looked up quickly. A pair of big gray rats was sitting on the beam a mere arm's length above him; if he reached out, he could touch them. They sat there quietly, peering curiously at him, sniffing at each other a little as if whispering together, and never taking their eyes off him. He could see distinctly their sharp white teeth. Nobody could have been here for a long time because the rats were completely tame.

He knew them all too well. In most of the houses the rats had eaten or destroyed everything edible. Even when people put their corn in large earthenware containers, the rats would get at it; and even if sausages and hams were hung from the roof, on the underside of large surfaces of wood, the rats would still win in the end. But this time he was lucky. Not very far from the smoke hole hung a big brown lump of something. If only it was something he could eat.

He clambered up on the large tabletop as a stepping-stone to the beams. "Some house this must be," he thought, "to have a table." Very few houses did—only Master Simon's, in fact, of those he had seen.

His hands and clothes were black with soot as he wormed his way up onto the beam. What a smell! But the brown lump *was* a ham, a good, big ham. He dropped it onto the earthen floor, making sure it landed with the brown rind downward. It did so, with a smack that echoed through the silent house. He was down after it like a flash.

Near the fireplace he caught sight of a long-bladed knife projecting from a crack in the beam. He went and pulled it out: he could use that. The wooden handle was polished with use. It was a strong, heavy knife.

He hurried out with his ham into the open air. He couldn't stand being cooped up in the empty house.

Out in the village street he sat down on a large stone and began carving the ham into mouthfuls. It was good! He chewed noisily as he ate—it was so long since anybody had told him to stop champing his food that he no longer gave it a thought. Rather salty! Never mind, it would last all the better, and he could eat every morsel. Now all he needed was some bread to go with it.

Back into the house he went again, to look for flour or bread. Bread was a rarity; the rats almost invariably got it, as they had done here. He searched on the shelves above the sleeping places, but there were only the rats' big, black droppings.

Perhaps there was some corn out in the barn? If so, he could grind it between two stones, or he could eat it just as it was. He had eaten many a grain of barley.

He went through the wicker door in the brushwood wall of the barn. The wall was daubed with mud to the height of the beams; above that level there was only wattle. Here, too, the floor was of earth. It was uneven, with hills, valleys, and in one place a miniature lake, the residue from the last spell of rain, no doubt.

On one side lay a pile of straw—a gray-looking heap, with a musty smell. From a beam a flail hung askew, as if whoever was threshing had had to hurry away and do something else. Somebody must have shouted to him, "Come here, quick!"

Next to the barn was the cowshed. The moment he went in, there was no mistaking the evil smell! He looked around to see where it came from.

"It must have been a calf," he said to himself. The horns were quite small. What was left of it lay over in a corner—bones, gristle, and the grayish skull with its horns. The rats had had a fine old feast.

He hurried out of the cowshed into the fresh air, where he stood and inhaled repeatedly. He had never really grown used to that smell. Many a time, when the stench of carrion had been too strong, he had stood and vomited until the tears came into his eyes, and his stomach had been sore for long afterward. Not that calves and other animals were the worst. Sometimes there had been people, too. And that was a hundred times worse.

He stood in the village street looking about him. The sun was about to set. The daily question arose: where was he going to sleep tonight? He had spent many nights under trees or among bushes, occasionally in a haystack, and sometimes in a barn when it was raining, but never in houses or farms, for before she died his mother had said, "Never sleep in empty houses; they have an evil smell!"

As he stood there, a new sound was borne on the air, as sudden and unexpected as a blow. He turned around so violently that the big knife he had fastened in his belt fell to the ground.

At first he thought he was dreaming; then it flashed through his mind that everything else was a dream: the weeks of loneliness, the journey through villages and forests. Another moment and he knew where he was and what he could hear. The church bell was ringing!

The sound was unmistakable. He could see the church from where he stood. The bell sounded feeble and cracked; it was evidently much smaller than the one at home in Ullsthorp.

Was it possible that this village was not quite deserted? Had the plague spared someone? Or was it the dead who had set the bell ringing?

He had heard that ghosts sometimes did things that had been left undone during their lifetime. Perhaps there were graves for which no bell had been rung? As a rule, when somebody died, the bell was rung for half an hour. Perhaps there had been too many for this to be possible.

Should he go to the church? He trembled a little at the thought. Still, if it were spirits who were ringing the bell, at least they couldn't be *evil* spirits. Evil spirits would have kept well away from the church.

Suppose it was a living person? Again, in that case it could not be an evil person. The house of God, the church, was a place of peace. Evil never went inside a church. It might lurk outside like a thick mist, but inside —never!

With slow movements he bent down and picked up the heavy knife. He weighed it in his hand for a moment before putting it back in his belt. Then he went up to the church.

CHAPTER 2

The young farm girl started up into a kneeling position. She must have fallen asleep.

She looked around confusedly, disappointment written all over her face. She rubbed her eyes and sighed.

Such a lovely dream she had had! She had been walking with Marie and Marta along a road that shone in the sunlight—a glorious road, where all the stones had turned into gold, beautiful round pieces of gold such as she had once seen belonging to a stranger who had stayed for a night in Claus Miller's house. As for the houses, they glittered and gleamed as if every brilliant color in the rainbow had fallen on them. From the most beautiful house she had ever seen there came the sound of a wonderfully happy song, as if all the stars in heaven were rejoicing together. Her eyes filled with tears.

And now she sat here! "Here" was the middle of a heap of hay—soft, fragrant hay that she herself had laboriously carried up here.

It was half dark as usual, but this she had soon

grown used to. The light came through a number of holes that the sparrows had made in the straw roof. Two of the shafts slanted down directly onto her heap of hay, like bright swords stretching down to her from the vault of heaven. It was always like this toward sunset.

Up under the roof, dusty cobwebs hung like huge gray curtains. She had pulled them down as far as she could reach—it was so disgusting to get them in her hair every time she went up to the loft. But whenever the wind played under the ridge of the roof, it was as if the place were alive up there.

In the hay alongside the girl was a cloth bag, and on the beam a gray leather bottle. She sighed again. To be sure, this was where she was. And Marie and Marta were gone.

She got up and went across to one of the sparrow holes in the roof. By standing on tiptoe she could see out over the churchyard as far as the two mounds down by the scrawny juniper tree that stood and kept watch. That was where it had ended for Marie and Marta.

She also had a bird's-eye view of the whole village and of the fields beyond. Today there was not an animal in sight. She had often seen animals, especially at the beginning. The cows used to wander out there; she heard their lowing and felt sorry for them—they needed to be milked. Once she had even seen a horse, but of late there had been very few animals. Presumably they had gone farther afield and into the forest.

Most of the animals, of course, had been put out to fend for themselves. Indeed, she had helped to set them free when Claus had realized how things were going for him.

At times she had believed that Claus would get better, but in her heart she had known differently all along. They had been the only ones left on the farm after Marta, Marie, the lad, and finally Mother Elsa had been taken out to the churchyard.

"Take a knife, Hanna," Claus had said, "and cut the ropes—unless you can untie the knots." Then he lay still for a long time before saying, "I'm at the end of the road now, Hanna. Our Lord is calling me home."

That was many days ago, so many that she had lost count. For a long time she had gone from farm to farm, but finally she had just stayed out in the field. Nobody had any use for her, so she had to fend for herself. She had come up here because she no longer dared to go into people's homes. People had become so afraid of each other—because of the plague.

Master Jacob had once said that you were safe in the house of God. She had remembered this, and that was why she had come up here one evening when it was raining heavily. Now it seemed as if she had been here for ages. It was better up here than down in the houses.

Master Jacob had made sure that none of the plague victims were buried under the floor of the church, where the gentlefolk were normally buried. Here there was never any smell of plague or death as there was in other places. Nor were there any church rats in Finthorp. Up here she could lie down and sleep in safety.

Through the holes in the roof she had seen many burials. At first people always sang, and Master Jacob would pronounce a blessing. As time went on, the singing grew weaker and weaker, until Master Jacob merely said a prayer. Finally it was just one or two people standing by the grave—in silence and with bowed heads.

Now it was many days since she had seen a soul in the village. No one had missed her—the orphan whom Claus Miller had brought up. In any case, she had stayed in hiding up here all the time.

When she could no longer see or hear anyone in the village, she had taken to ringing the church bell at sun rise and sundown. The dead ought to know that they were lying in the right ground.

Still she never saw a soul. Either everyone was dead, or the survivors had fled from the village. Perhaps there was still someone hiding in one of the houses from fear of the plague, but there was no means of knowing.

Nevertheless, every morning and every evening the little bell sent out its call over the land—the only living thing in a world that was dead as far as the eye could reach, a little flame of life and hope, a beacon calling to God and to other human beings.

When she peeped out of the hole in the roof, her eye fell on something unfamiliar in the village street: a living person!

Her heart beat faster. From where she was, she could not quite make out what kind of person it was. She screwed up one eye and gazed intently with the other. It was a stranger, that much she could see. Perhaps it was just a lad—he looked so small down there in the village street. The girl never took her eyes off him.

Now here was a problem: should she ring the bell when the sun went down? She was of two minds. She had always been afraid of strangers. Still, the lad looked so lonely, so harmless, standing down there in the deserted street.

There had been plenty to be afraid of; she had been afraid nearly all the time. It had been like going through a great forest where every tree meant a new fear. Now she had come out of the forest, on the other side. She no longer had the sensation of being afraid, not because she had ceased to care about anything, but because she knew that God was protecting her.

Hanna badly wanted to talk to somebody again. From time to time she had talked aloud to herself, up here in the loft—just a few words cast at random and upon the air. And she had often burst out singing songs and as much as she could remember of the psalms in Latin, if only to hear something, to drive the vast silence out of the church loft.

When the sun was almost touching the trees in the west, she descended the ladder into the body of the church. Then she walked slowly across to the west gable and took the bell rope off its hook. For a moment she stood still with the knot in her hands; then she pulled and the bell swung up over her head. It was green all over with verdigris, with white streaks of bird dung down the sides. "It's good to hear that sound," she thought.

Would the lad come? She was quite certain he would, but all the same she closed her eyes as she rang. She would stop at two hundred—and only then would she open her eyes to see if he was there. Her whole body tingled with excitement.

For the second time the boy scrambled up onto the stone wall. He wanted to see who was ringing the bell. It was strange hearing that sound again. He remembered the last time he had heard it, back at home. It was the very last thing he had done before setting out on his travels: to go to the church and ring the bell, loud and long, over the empty village.

Now he could see that it was a girl who was doing the ringing. What a surprise! For a moment he stood stock still. It had never occurred to him that a girl could ring a bell. At home it had always been Piers Bellman, while he was still alive. However, he decided to go into the churchyard.

As he got nearer, he could see that the girl ringer was facing the other way. In that case, he had better make a big loop around to the other side. He wanted to approach from in front. It was so frightening when people came up on you from behind without your seeing or hearing them. And that girl who stood there ringing the bell in a dead village had been frightened, badly and often. He was certain of that from his own experience.

When she had finished ringing, she opened her eyes, very slowly, as if to draw the excitement out a little longer. And there he was, right in front of her. She *was* just a bit frightened. He could see the fear in her eyes. Neither of them said a word.

The girl took the knot in the bell rope and fastened it securely in its hook on the wall. The rope must not be left to swing in the wind because it had to last for many years.

For what seemed to her like a long time, they just stood and looked at each other. During that time she took in everything about him, from the matted hair around the haggard, grimy face to the bare feet with their scratches and scars. Finally her gaze focused on the long knife tucked into his belt. She went on staring at that knife.

"You know how to ring a bell all right!" he said at last, slowly, as if disinclined to talk.

"He looks surly," she thought, not really a person to talk to. If only it had been a girl! All she said was, "Yes," accompanied by a serious nod.

After that they were both silent again. It was as if they needed to clear some obstacle between them, the exact nature of which they did not know. So they continued looking at each other, both of them interested, both of them on their guard.

A large fly buzzed around them. Suddenly it landed on the girl's nose. For a moment she took her eyes off the boy's face and squinted down her nose at the fly. She looked so funny that the boy was unable to contain himself. He began to laugh—at first only a little, but when the girl joined in, because the boy was laughing, he laughed all the more.

They stood by the church gable and laughed. They laughed so loud that the ravens took off from the roof of the church and flew across to the other roofs in the village.

"Is it always you who rings?" asked the boy, when he had finished laughing. He no longer looked so surly.

"I only do it because the others can't. They . . ." She broke off and looked in the direction of the gray mounds of earth. He followed her glance and understood everything.

She looked to be a sturdy girl, on the podgy side, with brown hair in a long pigtail and unusual eyes, dark and deep-set like those of a large wild bird he had once seen.

"Who are you?" she asked suddenly. She wanted to

talk with him, hear him talk, talk herself. It would not have surprised her if he proved to be descended from heaven, just so that she could have someone to talk to again after all the countless days she had been alone. But it was best to know who he was.

"Luke!"

He spoke as if addressing the air. He marveled at the sound of her light, girlish voice. He had almost forgotten what it sounded like when somebody talked, and hearing her gave him a lovely glow inside.

She looked questioningly at him.

Then it occurred to him that probably lots of people went around calling themselves Luke, so he added, "Luke Janson from Ullsthorp."

"I'm Hanna," she said, unprompted, "but they've always called me Claus Miller's little girl."

The boy nodded.

"Hanna!" He needed to savour the name—one he had never heard before.

"How . . ." he began, and then stopped. He was going to ask her how things were in this village, but he could just about see for himself. "I don't suppose there are any people still here? One or two perhaps?"

"People have gone away," she replied. "But most of them"—she indicated the graveyard with a sweep of the arm—"are with God."

He nodded again. His eyes became hard and stubborn.

She could see that he had suffered, that he had starved and wept and been very frightened. And suddenly it seemed as if she knew him well, as if she had always known him.

"It's the same at home," he said hurriedly, as if to get it over.

They seemed unable to get going; they both had too many private thoughts that they could not shake off.

The sun had gone down. It was a mild summer evening, in which mosquitoes hummed and a solitary blackbird, perched on the bell tower, poured its little melody out over the gray village. Another bird answered from somewhere among the gabled roofs.

"Come!" said Hanna, and she led the way into the church.

It was strange, being in a church at night. The door slammed with a bang that reverberated for a long time. It was half dark under the raftered ceiling.

From one corner a ladder led to a small rectangular opening, through which the thatcher used to crawl when the roof needed repairing. They climbed it, the girl leading, Luke slowly following.

"This is where I live," she said when they had reached the far end of the church loft.

He could hardly see a thing in the dark. All the way across the loft he had groped his way forward with outstretched arms. On one occasion he strayed over to the side where the cobwebs were. Now he stood trying to brush them off his face. The dust irritated his nostrils and made him sneeze. But he could smell the hay, and when he had stood and sniffed for a while, he could smell something else—a good and familiar smell.

"You live well here," he said into the darkness, and then sneezed.

"Are you hungry?" she asked the loft at large.

"I can't remember what it's like not to be hungry,"

said Luke, "but I can certainly remember what bacon and barleycorn taste like."

He felt his way forward, finally extracted the ham from his bag, and sat down in the hay beside the girl.

"That smells good," she said.

"So does your bread!"

And there they sat eating ham and bread.

Outside, the land lay waste. It was the beginning of a second life for them—life after the plague. Dimly they felt that this was an initiation. They ate in silence and drank ale from the girl's leather bottle.

"I'm tired," said Luke into the darkness as he stretched out on his back in the hay.

The girl answered in a cheerful voice, "You can sleep in peace here!"

"Are there rats?" he muttered.

"No, there are no church rats here—only stable rats, house rats, and kitchen rats galore. Here we can sleep in peace."

"It's a long time since . . ." said Luke presently. "I've mostly slept out of doors."

"Were you frightened?" she asked, not from curiosity, but because she had known fear herself and wanted to share the experience with the boy—since nothing is quite so frightening when you are no longer alone.

"Yes," he said simply. It had suddenly come home to him that tonight he could sleep without being frightened.

"I've always been frightened," said the girl. "But every evening I've said a prayer."

There was silence for a few moments; then she said in a low voice, "Do you think it matters if you cry when you pray to God?"

"There are things best said in the dark," she thought to herself, "where no one can see you."

"I've cried, too," said Luke as if from a great distance, "and . . . it doesn't matter."

"I'm glad you came," said Hanna, and the boy could hear the happiness in her voice.

"I'm going to thank God for sending you here."

Luke did not answer; he was asleep.

Suddenly Hanna felt afraid. Was everything really all right now? She could no longer hear the boy or see him. Had she dreamed the whole thing? Cautiously she stretched out her hand in the dark. Yes, there he was—she could feel his emaciated arm.

She folded her hands and smiled happily.

CHAPTER 3

"You're filthy!" said Hanna. She was subjecting Luke to a close inspection. In the morning light they could see each other properly for the first time.

"There's been very little water for washing where I've come from," he replied, "but I'll have a good wash when we come to a stream. I can't stand well water. There are often rats in the wells—or toads. Ugh!"

"We've a good stream in Finthorp," said the girl. "We'll go there."

Presently they came to the farmhouse Hanna knew so well. Inside were many barrels of ale, which was better to drink than water.

Hanna found Luke a leather bottle; he was thankful for that. Then they filled their bottles with the foaming ale.

Luke had plenty to be thankful for today—above all, for having found Hanna.

Back at the church they ate bread and ham and drank ale. But when Luke lay down for a bit in the grass behind the churchyard wall, he at once fell asleep. He slept all morning. And Hanna, realizing he must be very tired, let him sleep. She went around busying herself with this and that, but every now and then she went over to the wall to see if the boy was still there. It was after midday before he was awake and alert enough to talk.

First they made a tour of the village, with Hanna telling Luke who had lived in the various houses. Finally they came down to the stream. A short distance away was a large building straddling the water. "That's Claus Miller's mill!" announced Hanna. "I've often been here fetching corn and flour."

"Where did you get your bread from?" asked Luke.

"I baked it in the miller's oven; but that was when I still had plenty of fuel, and now there's hardly any left."

Luke was impressed by her cleverness. "Can you really make bread?" he asked, with a new respect.

Hanna laughed. If he only knew all the things a young girl learned to do at the miller's! "Oh, yes!" she said.

They clambered up the ladder into the millhouse, where the millstones were. Luke didn't know how the mechanism worked or how to get it going. Hanna showed him what to do; she had set her heart on fresh flour. "You have to tilt that bar," she said, pointing. "Then you raise the sluice gate."

But even when they joined forces and pulled with all their might, they couldn't shift the bar one inch, so they had to make do with the flour standing in a barrel. Luckily the rats had not yet gotten at it—there had been plenty for them to eat in the mill. Indeed, the place swarmed with rats, rustling and rummaging in every corner. Wherever Hanna and Luke looked, they could see traces of their activity.

Luke sat down on an empty barrel, his clothes white with flour dust. Hanna came and sat beside him. She was barefoot, like Luke, and wore a brown dress made of coarse cloth that reached to her knees.

Luke gazed at her reflectively. "What are you going to do now?" he asked, for Hanna had told him that she was all alone in her village.

"I don't know," she answered, shaking her head. "I suppose I'd better stay here. When people have stopped being afraid of the plague, perhaps some of them will come back. But I've also thought of going to another village and looking for other people."

"It's not so easy now," said Luke. "I've only been in one village in these parts where there were people; all the others were deserted."

"Couldn't you have stayed there?"

"I don't know—I never got right in."

"Why not?"

"They threw stones at me and shouted at me to hop it. They didn't want a scarecrow like me bringing the plague; they had enough already. 'Beelzebub's spawn' they called me—or something like that. It didn't sound friendly in any case. You can't stay in a village like that."

Hanna nodded; she knew it all. Here, too, people had been afraid; no one dared to open his door; sometimes they set the dogs on strangers. No doubt it was the same everywhere.

"Isn't there anyone you know?" asked Luke. "No relatives?"

She shook her head. "Claus Miller was only my guardian. Father and Mother died many years ago, when I was small. I've never known anyone outside this village, and now they're all gone—dead or gone away."

"Perhaps the ones who've gone away will come back—if they survive. At home I don't think there was anyone who went away. They nearly all died of the plague and were buried by Master Simon. He was one of the last to die."

"But where will you go now?"

"To my Uncle Nicholas."

"And where is he?"

"He lives at a place called Ribe. My father died, and when my mother caught the plague, she told us: 'Go to your Uncle Nicholas at Ribe. He's a good man, and the only man you can turn to. He's your father's brother, and after God he's your next best hope, if he's still alive.' "

"And are you going to . . . Ribe . . . now?" asked Hanna.

Luke nodded. "Yes. The others all died: Sven, Ester, and Ruth. I'm the only one left, so I have to go there by myself. It must be a long way to Ribe," he continued, "and I want to get there before the autumn, because then it's too cold to be out day and night."

"How will you find the way?"

"I don't know—I've never been away from home before. But I'm going to try, and I think I'll succeed."

"When do you mean to leave?"

"Tomorrow! And I have to keep going south, because then I'm on the right road. Ribe's supposed to be in the south—somewhere a long way away."

Hanna got up from the barrel and went over to the trapdoor. There she stood gazing in silence over the village.

Suddenly she went to another barrel and began eagerly ladling flour into her bag. The flour settled on her bare arms, and she was soon white up to the elbows. Without a word she took Luke's bag and filled that, too, with flour. Then she took her own bag, climbed down the ladder, and began walking along the stream.

Luke followed her for a little, but presently he stopped and turned to look back at the water mill, with its dam made of stones and turf. There was a sluice gate, which could be opened so that the water flowed against one side of the great horizontal wheel, whose vertical axle went right up into the millhouse and made the millstones turn.

Luke stripped and went into the water. It was good to get clean again.

When he emerged, he was unrecognizable. His face was a uniform brown, and his hands were almost white. Only his hair was more than he could manage: it was too long!

Hanna had returned and stood watching his attempts to comb it with his bare fingers. Luke glanced up at her. Her eyes were all red.

"Look," he said hurriedly, "couldn't you cut my hair? It's grown too long—far too long. Here, take my knife."

A little hesitatntly she took the long, heavy knife, weighed it in her hand, and then grasped it. A miller's girl is not used to handling things with kid gloves, and Luke grumbled and groaned under her treatment. With rapid strokes she cut off his hair in great handfuls, all the way around his head. And he thought how strange it was to have another living person near him.

"There we are," said Hanna at last. "I've finished." She stepped back a little and examined her handiwork. "You almost look like a decent human being," was her comment. "But wait a minute."

She took a comb from her pocket. "I'm going to comb you," she said. "You look like a haystack!" And she laughed a little at the thought of her combing Luke's hair. It was so matted that it took a long time. "Oh dear," she said, "now I've broken a tooth." Then she laughed again. At the sound of her laugh, Luke joined in.

Suddenly she stopped laughing, lay down in the grass, and hid her face in her arms. Her back heaved in a strange way.

Luke understood all too well what was happening to the girl. He stood watching her, uncertain what to do. He had never known what to do when somebody cried. If it had been his sister Ruth, he would first have teased her, then tried various ways of comforting her. But Hanna was another proposition. Besides, he didn't really know her yet.

Afterward Luke preferred not to think about what had followed, but it was a long time before they were able to continue. They both discovered, though, that the best way to comfort somebody who is crying is to cry yourself. And when the floodgates were about to burst . . .

"Never mind," said Luke finally, "you'd better come with me—you must, Hanna! You're all alone here, and I'm all alone. Will you come with me?"

"Yes," whispered the girl. "Yes, I'll come with you."

CHAPTER 4

In the morning they gathered up their bags and leather bottles and climbed down the ladder. The bags were bulging, the bottles heavy and so full that their gurgling was staccato and muffled. At the bottom of the ladder Luke stopped to fasten the leather strap on his bag, while Hanna laid her things on the floor. She walked cautiously and hesitantly across the floor of the church; the cold seeped up from the flagstones into her bare feet. Almost without a sound she went up to the altar.

She had often been here before when the church had been full of people; wooden clogs had clattered over the flagstones, and a murmur of voices had filled the church as they waited for Master Jacob. She could still hear the rustling of clothes and the heavy thud when the congregation knelt for prayers. Sometimes she had stolen glances at the rows of heads, all bowed except for the very old, who sat on broad planks against the walls and were excused from kneeling by reason of their stiff, rheumaticky legs—it would have taken too long helping them onto their knees and up again.

But today the building was vast and empty. She could almost be afraid of her own footsteps.

Luke followed Hanna and knelt with her before the altar, silent and pensive, praying. Then they went back through the church, and Hanna collected her things.

Luke shut the door and fastened the great oak bar: the animals must not go into the church, into the house of God. Nor must the wind tear the door off its hinges. Now there was no one in the village, only the animals and the wind.

They set off between the houses and out over the fields, overgrown now with weeds.

As they went, they exchanged experiences, learning to talk about them without tears, so that the two children suddenly found themselves chattering and laughing. Laughing! It was good to laugh again. From time to time they even played tag. The sun came out and scattered the clouds, and the day turned fine and warm.

At the edge of the forest they stopped for refreshment, looking back at the village as they ate. All they could make out was a little brown cluster, scarcely distinguishable from the surrounding greenery. The scattered bushes on the outskirts had had their lower branches gnawed by animals, so that you could see under them as if they were enormous green toadstools.

So far the going had been easy, but now the forest made it harder. In places there was thick undergrowth, and progress here was slow.

"Why can't we follow the road?" asked Hanna on one occasion when they had sat down on a mossy stone for a short rest.

"I did at first," said Luke. "I followed the wheel

tracks out of Ullsthorp. But I couldn't stand the people I kept meeting."

"You met people then?"

"Yes. Beggars, thieves, soldiers, people who'd left their homes . . . all of them inquisitive . . . wanting to know where you came from, where you were going, whether you were alone. Some of them even wanted to see what was in your bag. And if they could stomach it, they'd take it!"

But Luke said nothing about his biggest fear of all: the plague.

Hanna, too, was thinking about the plague, and she, too, preferred not to talk about it yet. It was as if they thought they could ward off the plague merely by keeping quiet about it.

And so they continued through the forest and the brushwood instead of following the ruts, where these were not yet hidden by grass.

Toward evening they emerged from the forest into a meadow. Here the only bushes were the kind that like water; otherwise, there were just tufts of rushes, grass, and a mass of different flowers.

They were pulled up short by a wide river—so wide that Luke was unable to throw a stone across, at the first attempt at least.

"What are we going to do now?" Hanna looked disconsolately at the gliding water.

"Can you . . . like that?" Luke waved his arms in front of him like a dog swimming while continuing to watch the water as it flowed gently away.

"Swim? No!" she said with a laugh. "I've never seen so much water at one time!"

"Neither have I! At home we only had a little stream, never deeper than you could easily stand up in—except in the spring when the snow melted, and then nobody felt like swimming."

"Couldn't we make a . . . something to cross over in?"

"A sailing ship? No, I don't think so. I've never seen one. How do people make them?"

"I don't know, but I've heard that people can."

They were tired, so they sat down on the riverbank and started eating. It was the only thing that helped and gave a little comfort when there was something wrong, as there nearly always was.

"I'll tell you what," said Luke with his mouth full of ham. "At home once they talked about a place where you could cross the river because the water wasn't very deep. A ford they called it."

"Where do you think it is?" Hanna's voice sounded tired.

He shrugged his shoulders. "It's either that way"—pointing east—"or the other way. Unless we meet somebody we can ask, we'll have to try our luck."

"Not today!" said Hanna. "I can't walk another step, my legs are aching so much."

"Well, we can't sleep here," said Luke. "We could easily fall in the water, or something might come out of the water—something dangerous. Hadn't we better go on a bit and find somewhere to sleep? I'm tired, too. How about over there," he said, pointing, "behind those bushes?"

So they continued, Hanna limping a little. It was slow going through the long reeds and little bushes.

"That was hard work!" said Luke, mopping his brow.

They had stopped beside the bushes, and there, straight ahead, were some haystacks—not very big ones, and just five of them.

"Here's where we're going to sleep!" exclaimed Hanna. She was off in a flash—without limping, Luke noticed. She ran all the way and threw herself onto the first haystack.

Luke, too, lay down in the hay. "You know . . ." he began, but that was as far as he got, because Hanna started pelting him with hay, and before he could get up or retaliate, she had practically buried him.

"Stop that," he growled as he fought his way out of the hay.

Hanna stopped as suddenly as she had begun.

"This can't be more than a fortnight old," he said.

"No, it's lovely and fresh," said Hanna, plucking hay from her hair. "That's why I couldn't wait to flop down in it. But surely it must mean there've been people here quite recently. Still, I don't think they'd mind if we slept here tonight."

"We won't ask," said Luke, "because there's nobody in sight, and if you don't ask, there's nobody to say no!"

They lay talking for a little longer. When the sun went down, the evening turned chilly. The gray night mist began to spread, rising from the water and drifting out over the meadows on either side of the river, like steam from a great cauldron simmering on the hearth. The two children dug themselves deeper into the haystack for warmth. They were dead tired and soon fell fast asleep.

Hanna was awakened by something or other pricking her neck, a dead thistle perhaps. Then she realized she was shivering with cold. When she opened her blue eyes, she found herself looking straight into the moon's yellow one. It looked as if a net had been draped over it. She groped for a moment in the hay, then sat up to see better. It was almost as if the mist were water and the bushes were islands dotted around in it. A strange light, as of bright silver, filled the entire world.

But somewhere behind the shimmer and the mist there was a curious noise. At first it was so faint that she was not certain if it really was a noise. But suddenly it was beyond doubt. She could hear something out there: a rustling, creeping sound that sent a shiver all the way down her spine.

What should she do? Should she wake the boy, sleeping so snugly in the haystack? In the strange light she could see no sign of him.

Yes, perhaps the best thing would be to wake him. She was a little frightened. Cautiously she reached out with one hand and touched his shoulder. Then she shook it a couple of times. It made no difference; he did not move.

She could still hear something rustling out there. Wolves? The stealthy steps approached from several directions at once. There were shufflings and snufflings, inhalings and exhalings, audible quiverings of nostrils.

She shook Luke again, roughly and repeatedly. And still he went on sleeping. If only she dared, she would have called to him, shouted in his ear, forced him to wake up. She gave him yet another shove.

Now she could dimly make out some gray shadows in the mist, and still he slept. He even started making little snoring noises every time she shook him.

She pushed him as hard as she could in the position she lay, only just able to reach him. Luke stirred, turning heavily in the hay and emitting a high-pitched nasal sound—a kind of snore. Then he settled down again, but continued to growl and snarl in his sleep.

The effect was immediate: the shaggy gray shadows in the mist at once stopped advancing. Another moment and they had disappeared from Hanna's view. For a little while she could still hear their noises in the distance. Then all was still.

Hanna lay motionless. She heard the sound of many feet over the meadow, like a danger receding from her. And now she gave up trying to wake Luke. "If he wants to sleep, let him sleep," she said to herself. She lay still as a mouse, her ears cocked in the gray moonlit night. What was afoot—or underfoot? Was it goblins and pixies who had emerged from their underground lairs? Either that or wolves. They'd better not come back! Hanna resolved to stay awake and keep watch for them.

She must have fallen asleep all the same, for suddenly she became aware of Luke standing beside the haystack, stretching himself. It was broad daylight, the sun shone, and the birds sang.

Hanna stuck her head out of the hay and peered at Luke.

"You're full of hay!" she said.

He laughed. "You're a regular haystack yourself," he teased, "and a very sleepy haystack at that."

Suddenly she remembered. "If you knew," she said, "you'd soon take that grin off your face." She crawled out of the haystack, brushed her clothes down with her hands, and started pulling hay out of her hair.

"What are you talking about?" he asked.

"You could have been eaten alive—without even knowing it, the way you were sleeping—by a whole pack of wolves!"

"That doesn't sound too good," said Luke. But he didn't seem to Hanna exactly terrified. "They can't have been very hungry, though," he continued. "Look!" And he pointed at something at the other side of the haystack.

From where she stood she could see nothing. But when she went over to him, she looked and saw a short distance away a flock of sheep grazing peacefully in the meadow.

"I expect the wolves have gorged themselves on mutton!" said Luke. "That must be why they had no appetite left for a skinny fellow like me!" He spoke quite seriously, but she thought she glimpsed a mocking gleam in his eye.

The whole episode ended with their both laughing and chatting about wolves and sheep as they ate a hearty breakfast. After breakfast they continued on their way.

"The sensible thing to do is to go east," said Luke, "because that way the river's getting narrower all the time—to the west it's getting wider until it flows into the sea a long way away. And if we stay here, we'll soon meet people, because where there are haystacks there are people. Haystacks don't grow up of their own accord."

"No," said Hanna, "and where there are sheep, there are shepherds."

"Are you afraid of meeting people?" asked Luke, in a

tone which implied that he at any rate was not afraid.

"No, I don't think so . . . only of the plague." She stopped, and it was as if the word *plague*, like an unripe sloe in autumn, had made her purse up her lips.

"The plague is the will of heaven," said Luke solemnly. "That was what Master Simon always said whenever there was a burial, and sometimes there were two or three in a day."

"It's true," said Hanna. "The old grandma at Claus Miller's was born on a Sunday, and so she could see a lot of things that other people can't see."

Luke nodded. "I've heard that said about people born on a Sunday. But I've never met a real Sunday's child."

"It's true," repeated Hanna, "because Grandma Miller used to say, even before the plague started, 'I've seen things,' she'd say. 'May God protect and help us!' But for a long time she wouldn't say what it was she'd seen because it was so awful. But in the end she told me because I too am a Sunday's child."

"Are you? Can you too . . . ?"

Hanna didn't answer; she just looked into Luke's eyes and went on with her story.

"Grandma was so old that her hands shook. She couldn't even eat her soup. Somebody always had to help her with her food and drink, and I was the only one who had time. I did the things others didn't have time for. You see, I could simply get up a little earlier or go to bed a little later.

"She told me many things, Luke. And once she told me what it was she'd seen. 'I saw it clearly with my own eyes,' she said. 'I saw a man so tall that his face was hidden by clouds, and I could see his legs and part of his body. His legs were like great big old trees, only they shone like copper. It was Saint Michael himself in full armor. Then he drew his sword from its sheath and pointed with it over the land. Then he continued on his way, pointing at houses, towns, and villages. And that is how I know a plague is coming. The whole land will be emptied of people. It will be the worst death the world has ever known.'

"That was what she said," Hanna concluded.

Luke gazed thoughtfully in front of him. "That was a strange story," he said. "What do you suppose people have done? Have they all been so wicked?"

"That wasn't the reason, according to Grandma Miller. I mean, that men were wicked. 'You're certainly no worse and no better than anyone else, my child—than Marie or Marta or any of the others. But, my child,' she said, stroking my head with her trembling hand, 'I can see that you are going to be the only one left in our village—when all the rest of us are gone!' "

"And what did you say to that?" asked Luke.

"Yes, what did I say?" Hanna sighed. "I shook my head and said that now Grandma must eat her soup. What else could I say? What would you have said if somebody had told you that you were going to be the only person left in Ullsthorp?"

"I wouldn't have believed him."

"But she just put her wrinkled hand on my arm and said she knew because she had seen it." Hanna hesitated a little, as if uncertain whether to continue. "And she said

I would meet somebody my own age and would set out on a long and very difficult journey. She said something else, too." Hanna stopped abruptly.

"What was that?" Luke had become curious.

"She said . . . she said . . . oh, I don't know. Yes . . . she said I had the sign on my forehead!"

"That wasn't what you were going to say!"

"No . . . yes . . . I don't know. But what did she mean by a sign on my forehead? I've looked for it every time I've seen my face in the water. Can you see anything?" Hanna turned toward Luke and looked him straight in the eye. Then she pushed back her hair from her forehead with both hands.

Luke could only see her freckled face and a pair of large eyes looking seriously at him. But he could not bear all this talk about the plague and other misfortunes. He would much rather they forgot the whole business and laughed a little.

He peered solemnly at Hanna's freckled face. She had such a funny little nose and eyes that easily filled with life and laughter. If only she would laugh!

"Yes," he said at last.

"What can you see?" Hanna whispered.

"It's hard to say." Luke's voice, too, had sunk to a whisper. "I don't know if I dare tell you." He drew a deep breath as if it cost him a great effort. "I can see that you've rubbed your forehead with dirty hands, and I can see that you haven't washed properly!"

She gave a little cry of disappointment. "You're just like Claus Miller's lads; they were always teasing me." But she laughed all the same. "It was good that you came to our village," she said.

"It was because I had to go south to my uncle at Ribe," said Luke.

They continued for a little in silence. "Look!" shouted Hanna suddenly. "There—that must be where the shepherd lives."

CHAPTER 5

For a moment they stopped in their tracks, staring ahead over the bushes. For some time they had abandoned the riverbank, and now they were standing on top of a low hillock. The going was easier here because the ground was hard and firm, whereas down by the river it was often soft and marshy.

From the hillock they could see a small building a little way off in the meadow—a small gray building with mud walls and a thatched roof. Outside there was a large enclosure made of stakes and branches; this must certainly be for the sheep. But what riveted their attention was a thin wisp of smoke rising vertically into the clear blue sky.

They stood in deep silence until Hanna said, "There's someone living there!"

It suddenly occurred to them that this was the first time since they had been together that they had met another human being. They had almost begun to feel they were the only people in the whole world. And now they had a great longing to talk to somebody.

"What shall we do?"

"We could go and see if they'll let us cook some food," said Luke. He was thinking of all the handfuls of hard barleycorn he had eaten—and of all the tough mouthfuls of ham he had gnawed in the last day or two. It would be lovely to bake some of the ham and make some fresh bread.

"Yes," said Hanna, "I suppose I could bake some bread." Then it all came back to her, and she became anxious. "But suppose they won't have us—won't even let us in?"

"In that case we can go away again," said Luke. "Run, if we have to. Perhaps they'll tell us where we can find a ford. If we know that, we can manage the rest for ourselves."

"If only they're not too frightened!" said Hanna with a sigh. It was hard to accept the idea that they had to be frightened about whether people would be frightened of them.

At all events there was somebody at home. A woman emerged from the house even before they reached it.

"Have you got the plague?" She shouted so loud that they could hear her words a long way off.

"No, praise be to God," answered Hanna promptly. "And we're all on our own and on our way to Uncle Nicholas at Ribe!"

"Ribe? Heaven help us!" said the woman. "Come in here then!"

"Thank you," they said as they came up to the house. It was not big and had only a single room. In fact, it was not really a house but only a hut such as shepherds live in when they are out with the animals.

"Are you hungry?" asked the woman when they had gone into the hut.

They both nodded without taking their eyes off her. She was tall and broadly built and wore a brown skirt reaching to her ankles. Above it she had on a sleeveless sheepskin jacket, which had once, no doubt, been white but was now more like gray. Her muscular arms were bare and brown all over from the sun and the wind or the smoke from the hearth—almost like a pair of smoked hams!

She looked strong, capable of carrying a sheep under each arm. Her thick, dark hair was gathered in a long braid at the back, and her face was broad and coarse, with sharp eyes that looked searchingly at the two children like a hawk watching a pair of mice.

"Yes, but we've got food with us," said Hanna. "Perhaps we could roast some of our meat and bake a . . ."

"That you shan't," said the woman. "If you're going all the way to Ribe, you'll need all your food. You can stay here and have some of my food."

Her voice was rough, almost like a man's.

"How far is it to Ribe?" asked Luke eagerly.

"That I can't tell you. I've never been there, but sometimes I've heard passersby talk of Ribe. They always said it was a goodly distance. But now you're going to have some food."

Presently they were sitting on the ground, each with a wooden mug in one hand and a hunk of fresh barley bread in the other.

They drank the warm soup with relish. Afterward they ate some smoked mutton until their whole faces gleamed with fat, and all the time they took turns in telling the shepherd's wife where they came from, where they were going, and how the plague had raged everywhere they had been.

In exchange they learned that the shepherd and their son Jacob were out watching the sheep.

They had collected the sheep from many villages round about, the woman explained, for since the plague there were many sheep with no owners and nobody to look after them. They were quite defenseless against wild animals, and so they were looking after them here, far from any village. Before the plague they had only had a small flock, but now they had many hundreds of sheep to care for. They had never dreamed there could be so many sheep in the world.

The plague hadn't reached them out here in the meadows, and they had scarcely seen another soul during the last year. When it was all over, his lordship on the royal estate would doubtless take possession of the sheep, but until then they would look after them—and get food from them, added the woman.

"We've been told there's a ford somewhere near here," said Luke, who was thinking ahead. "Do you know where it is?"

Yes, she could certainly tell them that. But she didn't think they'd be able to find it themselves. "Tomorrow our boy is going that way with some sheep. There are too many of them," said the woman with a crafty look. "He's going to try and sell some to a man from the east. And if you don't mind waiting till tomorrow, Jacob can show you the way, and then you'll have no trouble crossing the river. He's a good boy," she added, for she could see them looking thoughtful. She also told them that a flock of sheep had wandered away and could not be found.

It at once occurred to Hanna that these must be the sheep that had frightened her in the night. "We've seen them," she said. "We could fetch them for you, couldn't we, Luke?"

Luke agreed. "If we really can't find the ford for ourselves, we may as well do something useful while we're waiting."

"In exchange for the food!" added Hanna.

So the rest of the day went in fetching home the missing sheep. It was easy enough to find them again, but it was infernally difficult getting them to go home. By evening they were both worn out from spending the whole afternoon running and jumping after the sheep.

That night they were allowed to sleep in a corner of the hut. Hanna folded her hands and thanked God for helping them to find a safe place to sleep in. Luke lay wondering how far they had to go before they came to Ribe. Would they find the way? Would they last out? Was Uncle Nicholas still alive?

All these questions whirled around in his head while Hanna slept and the snores of the shepherd's wife wafted across to him from the other wall. Outside the hut he could hear the sheep moving around.

As yet there was no sign of Jacob or his father. He hoped they weren't going to have to wait here for several days.

In the morning Luke woke to find an enormously tall, enormously broad man standing there peering curiously at them.

Luke closed his eyes again. When you have a nightmare, the thing to do is to try and wake up, and then the nightmare will go. And if you dream that you're awake, the thing to do must be to try to go to sleep again. Luke tried at any rate, hoping the dream would vanish.

But a moment later, when he again opened his eyes a fraction, he knew beyond doubt that he was fully awake. The giant was stirring a pot over the fire. The woman was nowhere in sight.

Luke must have made a noise that the giant heard. He squinted up from his pot, and when he saw Luke, he straightened up to his full height. His head was right up between the rafters, but Luke could make out a great beard reaching far down over his broad chest. "A suitable husband," Luke thought, "for such a big woman."

"Well, well," said the giant, "the little lambs are waking up. Come, my lambkins, come and get some milk from mother!" He clucked with his tongue and chuckled to himself, and finally he laughed so loud that Hanna woke and sat up. Terrified by what she saw, she ducked down again and huddled close behind Luke's back.

At this moment the woman came in. She must have been out with the sheep because she was carrying a wooden pail full of milk. She looked from the man to the pair in the corner and back again.

"What's all this?" she asked. "You're not afraid of Jacob, are you? I told you he was a good boy! Now don't stand there, boy, looking as if you wanted to eat the poor mites. Say good morning nicely and make them feel welcome. They're our guests—and they've found the twenty sheep that you lost!"

Jacob muttered to himself, and afterward they squabbled over what he had said. Luke thought it was something about a wagon or a flagon, while Hanna was quite certain it was something about a *dragon*.

They laughed a little, but not too loud, because never in all their lives had they seen such an enormous "good boy."

When Jacob and his mother had both gone out, Hanna whispered, "What do you suppose the father looks like? I mean when the son is so huge."

"I can't imagine," said Luke. "But Jacob could be that size just by taking after his mother. I've never seen such a woman before. Perhaps it's because they've had plenty to eat all the time. Because if you eat a lot, you get bigger and bigger, and they've certainly had more to eat than ordinary farmers."

"You could say it's the plague they've grown big and fat on!" said Hanna. "It's the plague that's brought them all those sheep."

Later in the day they set out with the shepherd "boy" Jacob along the river. They had fastened their bags extra securely, for they had become much heavier and bulkier after the shepherd's wife had borrowed them for a while.

So now they were heading east with Jacob at a leisurely pace since the sheep seemed reluctant to stir themselves in the warm weather. Jacob himself led the way, with the sheep following obediently if slowly. A gray dog, more like a wolf, brought up the rear.

At midday Jacob stopped to let the sheep graze a little and drink from the river. At this point a road was clearly discernible, coming from the north and leading down to the riverbank. It had gradually come into being through a series of people driving their oxcarts in the tracks of those who had gone before. If the ruts became too deep or jolty, people drove a little to one side instead, so that the road consisted of five or six sets of tracks side by side. Here it was impossible to make out how many wheel tracks there were because they all merged as they approached the water, where they ended.

"There it is!" said Jacob.

"There what is?" Hanna looked at the sheep, which had drunk their fill and were now mostly engaged in nibbling the grass.

"The ford!" Jacob pointed across the river. "Just aim for that little bush over there, and you'll have no trouble."

Now Hanna and Luke could see that the wheel tracks continued on the other side of the river. They surveyed the scene. To the east stood a clump of trees in the middle of a flat stretch of meadow. They were not part of the forest, which started a good deal farther back from the river, so far away that the river never reached it, not even in the spring floods.

Hanna and Luke could also make out buildings on the other side.

"What's that?" asked Luke, pointing.

"That's the royal estate;" answered Jacob. "Once, you know, it was full of huntsmen and all kinds of folk. Now it's empty."

"Yes, but oughtn't you to take the sheep there?"

"Ay," answered Jacob with a grin, "but not just yet, and not to his lordship. Not likely! He's dead and buried, the beast! But there's another man I've come across," continued Jacob, still grinning, "a . . . er . . . a kind of merchant, you might say. He's going to take the sheep east. We mean to get some payment for all the trouble we've had with those sheep, and once there's a new master on the estate, it'll be too late. And that won't be long now."

"What will you get for them?" asked Hanna.

"See here!" Jacob produced a large leather purse and held it out for them to see. It was filled with silver coins. "Help yourselves," he said. And when they showed no sign of doing so, he counted out twenty shining pieces of silver. "That's one for every sheep you found yesterday," he said, "and that's what I expect to get for them. But don't you go and blab that I'm selling sheep in these parts," he concluded with another grin.

"And take good care of the money. You'll need it before you get to Ribe. Never let nobody see you've got money on you. It's good to have money, but it can be dangerous, too!"

Luke thanked him and took the gleaming coins. "Do you know how far it is to Ribe?" he asked. "I mean, how many days will it take us?"

"That I can't say," answered Jacob. "It depends on how fast you can go. There's a lot more rivers to cross. I know there are folk who do it in a week, but they're used to it and know the way. Ribe is the first real town you come to. You can see the cathedral a long way off. They say you can see it from more than a day's journey away."

"A week," thought Luke. "That will mean at least ten days for us."

Hanna took the silver coins and tied them up in her scarf so that they would be safe in her pocket. "We ought to hide them a bit better, but we can do that later," she said.

"How?" Luke spoke without thinking. His mind was on the way to Ribe, wondering whether they should follow the road since that was certainly the simplest.

"Why, sew them into our clothes, or make a bag for them and hang it on a string around the neck, or something."

"It's an easy crossing here," said Jacob, pointing across the river. "I grant you it's the widest part, but if you remember to make straight for that bush over there, you'll be all right."

"Can we touch the bottom easily?" asked Hanna.

"Oh, ay, it's only waist deep. Ah, but you should see it in winter. Why, there's often so much water, you can hardly see the other side. You don't want to try and cross then. . . . But off you go now, and next time you want Sheep-Jack, as they call me, you know where to find me!"

"But we'll be wet through," said Hanna.

"Take your clothes off," said Jacob. "That's what I always do." They glanced quickly at each other. At home they always undressed before crawling under the blankets and thought nothing of others being there, but this was different. They still didn't really know each other.

A little later they were on their way across, their clothes tied up in bundles, which they supported on their heads with one hand. The water was by no means unpleasant. Indeed, it was rather nice to cool off in this hot weather.

When they got to midstream, they had to tread carefully. The water rose until it reached their chins, and the strong current swirled against their legs. They held hands tightly to avoid being swept off their feet. After a while it began to get less deep.

"Whew," said Luke with a grunt. "Waist deep that was supposed to be—it must have been Jacob's waist! I daresay he forgot we're only the normal size!"

Soon they reached the other bank, where they put down their bundles and ran about in the meadow until they were dry. Their bodies were absolutely white, for the sun never reached beyond their faces, arms, and legs.

As soon as they were dressed, they continued on their journey. Before setting off along the wheel tracks to the south, they waved good-bye to Jacob, who in the meantime had rounded up his sheep and was now on his way again.

For the rest of the day they followed the tracks south. The meadow was absolutely flat, and they counted on seeing people a long way off.

"We'll have plenty of time to hide if anyone comes," said Luke.

"Why, do you think they'll do anything to us?" Hanna asked in alarm. "Jacob and his mother were as nice as could be."

"Oh, they may be harmless, but you never can tell. You meet all sorts on the road, not just villagers. Villagers we know. It's not them we need to be afraid of."

They walked all day, and when evening came, since the weather was fine, they simply lay down for the night in a thicket just off the road. The next morning they ate a hearty meal from the food the shepherd woman had given them: a couple of good, salty salamis, a whole leg of mutton, and two large round loaves of bread. For water they could drink from streams on the way and fill up their leather bottles.

Once more they set out on their way. As before, the

landscape consisted of willow scrub and bushes of bog myrtle, alternating with heath and stretches of meadow crossed by streams. But they did not pass another human being, or even a house.

As time went on, their conversation began to dry up. It was strange being so remote from mankind, and since it was a scorching hot day, they were sweating and footsore. Luke, indeed, was limping badly, for he had cut his foot on a sharp flint in jumping up on a tuft that turned out to be a stone.

Thus, their progress across the monotonous landscape slowed down considerably.

Far ahead they could make out a black bump on the horizon, a molehill on the endless plain, and kept it in sight for several days, until the bump proved to be a hill with a clump of gnarled oaks on top. They climbed the hill, which gave them an excellent view over the countryside through which they had limped day after day. On the other side, to the south, the landscape was very different. There were trees and, at the foot of the hill, a series of green fields and a little village.

Luke had found walking very difficult for the last two days and was now talking almost to himself as he sat nursing his swollen foot.

"Dare we go down there?" asked Hanna. "Or shall we go around?"

"We must rest. I can't go on with this wretched foot, but I don't know if we can risk going into the village."

Here it was again: something invisible speaking to them—fear of the plague, fear of strange places and strange people. They remained silent. Hanna moved a little closer to Luke as they sat on the grass.

It was the weather that decided the matter. The sky was growing overcast above their heads, and they heard a rumble somewhere in the distance. Warm gusts of wind kept blowing across the land. The sun disappeared in a veil of clouds that had gathered imperceptibly.

"Hadn't we better go down there?" asked Hanna, with a glance at the sky. "I can't bear thunder."

"Yes, but . . ." Luke muttered something as he got up with great difficulty.

"The church!" said Hanna simply.

"Ah, yes," thought Luke. "She feels the same as I do."

"There's nothing there, in the church, no plague and no bad people," she said. "Shan't we go down there? At least until the thunderstorm is over? It's going to be a bad one."

Luke began limping down the hill.

CHAPTER 6

The church door was unlocked. Long before they reached it, they could see that it stood ajar, as if the village's last inhabitants had been in such a hurry to get away that they hadn't had time to close the door behind them. The churchyard was full of mounds. Some were almost gray and bare, but most of them were overgrown with grass and weeds.

The church was built of rough granite blocks, with walls thick enough to withstand the last trumpet. But Luke noticed that the roof was only of heather—a poor roof.

They went inside and fell silent. Their slow steps echoed throughout the building, which was like other churches they had been in. Just inside the door was the heavy font, laboriously hewn out of an enormous stone. A face looked at them from each of the font's sides, a stern face that one would gladly hide from. This was where babies were christened; no wonder they began to howl as they were dipped in the water.

Hanna peered into the font. There was still water in it, water so dark that she couldn't see the bottom, but it reflected the rafter ceiling and her disheveled head.

On the wall hung a great picture of Christ on the cross, life-size and painted in strong colors. The crown of thorns was a lurid green, and the places where the nails had pierced the feet and hands were bright red with blood. Ahead of them, they saw that the altar consisted of two stones supporting a third, bigger than the others.

There was no ladder up to the loft, so they sat on the stone step by the open door. From here they could see the village, which looked like the other few villages they had seen in the course of their lives—a small, poor collection of seven or eight cottages, their roofs made of heather, which over the years had taken on the same gray color as the earth.

"It's obvious there's nobody here," murmured Luke as he began eating the bread that Hanna offered him. "So we shan't know how far it is to Ribe."

They sat there eating and all the time watching the clouds gather over the village like thick, black eiderdowns. The sun had vanished; it was twilight in midafternoon. Flies and midges buzzed over the churchyard. There was a deadly calm.

"I'm glad we've got a roof over our heads," said Luke, "because that black sack up there is going to start leaking soon." He jerked his head in the direction of the clouds.

"You should never point at a thunderstorm."

Hanna sat combing her long hair. Now at last she had a chance to do so, and the mirror made by the black water had made her realize how untidy she looked.

"Are you afraid?" she asked.

"Master Simon always said . . . always said . . . told us it was God who sent the thunder and lightning. And if we're in His house, He won't strike us."

But suppose He decided, nevertheless, to strike Hanna and Luke here and now—what then?

That was hardly likely. Luke was positive. "He would never let us escape the plague and come all the way here and then think, 'Now I've got them. Now I can strike them with lightning.' He doesn't play with us!" Luke thought of a cat toying with a mouse before killing it.

No, that seemed to make sense. Hanna gave a sigh of relief.

All the same, they moved back into the church a moment later when there was a violent clap of thunder.

Luke clambered up on the stone bench that stood along the outer wall. From here he could just about reach up to the bottom of the window. "Come and have a look," he said. Hanna climbed up on the bench with him and peered out.

They could see a large segment of sky and every roof in the village—and a cluster of large gray mounds around the church.

It started to rain. They jumped down again, for the rain had started coming in on them through the window. At one time this had been protected by hogs' bladders; they could still see the remains.

There were two other similar windows, but over by the altar there was another kind—one made of glass. Countless pieces of colored glass formed a picture. They sat for a long time gazing at it.

"Look," said Hanna, "it's a man!"

At first Luke was unable to see the man, but Hanna explained. "He's leaning forward a little—he's doing something—reaping, I think. He's using a scythe."

And now Luke, too, could see him: Death with his scythe!

Outside, the thunder had grown worse. A gust of wind drove spouts of rain in through the windows, making a large wet patch on the stone floor in front of each.

Hanna drew Luke over to the altar, where they stood for a while, huddled together. Hanna closed her eyes and began praying. But nothing lasts forever, neither happiness nor sorrow nor fear. Everything comes to an end.

"Amen!" concluded Hanna. "Now I am sure that nothing will happen to us here in God's house!"

Luke just nodded.

The rumble of thunder was more distant now. Luke climbed up on the bench again and squinted out of one of the narrow windows. Watching him closely, Hanna thought that he had opened his eyes wider than usual.

"What is it?" she asked.

"There's smoke rising from one of the cottages," he said. He sounded quite out of breath. "From the smoke hole!"

"But in that case . . . in that case there must be people there, living people. Shan't we . . ." She stopped, for now there were other things than the thunderstorm to think about.

Luke still stood there, gazing out. "We'll stay here until the thunderstorm's over."

A little later he said, "I'm certain the plague is finished here. Look! None of the graves is new; they nearly all have grass or weeds on them."

At that moment the lightning flashed, a sharp sword of fire cutting across the sky. The thick walls seemed to quiver in the thunder.

Luke leaped down from the bench—or perhaps he was pushed. "That struck!" he said as soon as he was able to make himself heard.

"It's God who sends the lightning," said Hanna firmly. She had said those words many times—more often than she could remember—but they helped her to forget her fear.

For a while the lightning continued to rake the sky in sudden, sharp flashes, causing strong shadows to leap out in the church. The thunder crashed; the rain pelted down.

Presently the thunder died away, and the rain stopped. The two refugees stood in the doorway again and looked out at the world.

The farm at the other end of the village was on fire! It made a mighty blaze, like a great pillar of fire with a crown of black smoke. The wind had died away, so that the flames rose straight into the air. They could hear quite distinctly the crackling noise of the fire, like a continuous shower of pebbles, as the thunder moved farther and farther east, over the forest.

"Come on," said Luke. "I've never seen a farm on fire."

"I have," said Hanna. "It's a dreadful sight." She began telling him about it, though she could hardly bear to think of the charred remains: cows, calves, and pigs. But Luke was already gone.

By the time they got near, the farm was burned almost to the ground. The flames were lower now, and the whole building had collapsed, leaving only a white-hot heap of straw and beam ends. They could feel the heat from some way off. The roof of the nearest farm was steaming strongly, though the soaking it had received from the rain had prevented it from catching.

They had eyes only for the fire, but suddenly Hanna gripped Luke's arm hard. "Look," she whispered.

Luke looked where she was pointing and saw a man —an old man with long white hair and a gray beard. He was sitting on an upturned barrel opposite the burned farm. His clothes were ragged, and he wore a red pixie cap. He had evidently not yet seen them, absorbed as he was in contemplating the ruins of the farm. He was so near, however, that he was bound to see them sooner or later, and shortly, through the crackle and roar of the fire, they heard him shout.

"Hi, there!"

He kept his eyes on them as he shouted. Then he beckoned to them, a slow, weary movement, as if it were all he had strength left for.

"Hi, there!" he called again, and they approached him, Luke leading the way.

"*Puh!*" The old man spat—first toward the fire, then toward the approaching children. "Sanrock, Beelzebub, and Lucifer, abracadabra, avaunt!" he intoned as they came nearer. At the same time he swung his arms in front of him in great circles, as if to sweep his two visitors away.

"They've burned my farm, burned it to ashes," he said fiercely. "I saw them with my own eyes. They rose up out of the blackness of hell, when the thunder rolled and the earth gaped!

"It's true!" he shouted suddenly, as if someone had contradicted him. But Hanna and Luke just gazed at him in silence.

"Yes, they came, all three of them. Lucifer in front, riding on a burning stake, then Sanrock, leaping about till the bells in his fool's cap jingled, and Beelzebub in the rear. He's their prince; the others are only his outriders."

The two children crossed themselves. It was horrifying to see the old man sitting outside his burned farm and hear him naming the evil spirits.

"Don't you . . . don't you . . . think," stammered Luke, "that it . . . it was the thunder, the lightning, that struck your farm?"

"But I saw them!" The old man shouted so loud that the silent village reverberated.

Suddenly Hanna noticed that the old man had only one leg. The other ended just below the knee. She tried to imagine how it would look if it was a complete leg—and thought it would end in a horse's hoof.

"The plague spared me—spat me out like a rotten plum! All the others have gone, under the earth, or fled to another hell or another heaven!

"But I know, I know *her!*" he shrieked. "It's *she* who's sent them, to burn my farm with their brands from hell! Otherwise, why should it only be *my* farm? All the other farms are empty! Oh yes, they know where to strike all right! The empty farms are still standing. The only one where there's life is struck!"

The old man looked sinister as he sat there shouting.

He turned up the whites of his eyes as he cursed all the dead—and the living who had fled from the village—but most of all "her," she who according to him had sent the evil ones to burn him up—him, the only person the plague had spared in the whole village!

Hanna crossed herself each time he named the evil names. One never knew what might happen when a madman invoked the evil spirits by name.

"Couldn't you live in one of the other farms?" asked Luke cautiously. "They're all empty. As you say, they're either dead or gone away."

"What!" shouted the old man, shaking his fists. "Do you expect me to live there—where they are sure to come back as ghosts and visit me in the night? You see that farm?" He pointed at the steaming farm next door. "Piers lived there! Do you expect me to live in Piers's miserable rat's-nest of a farm? Piers cheated and twisted us all, in every way you can think of. And you expect me to live there? No, thank you! No, thank you! I'd rather rot out here under the open sky!

"And do you suppose it would be any better at Lars's farm? If anyone ever had reason to come back, it was Lars! He was a swine! You wouldn't believe the things he did when he'd drunk too much ale—as he always did! The whole village could have drowned in the ale that man must have drunk. And more than once he's killed a man when he was drunk. Do you think I want him coming back and glowering at me with his beery eyes while I'm asleep? Never!

"Or Matthew? He'll come back, too, as sure as eggs is eggs! Why, he's even perjured himself. With my own ears I heard him swear he had no silver, and with my own eyes I've seen him bury it at the edge of the wood, where it's still lying. And if any people come back after they're dead, perjurers do!"

"Yes, but . . ." said Hanna when the old man had paused for breath in the recitation of his neighbors' characters. "Yes, but weren't there any decent, honest folk living here? A pretty little village like this—wasn't there a single poor soul honest enough for you to believe he's at peace in his grave?"

Hanna gazed at the old man with her big, serious eyes; she was beginning to forget who and where she was —that she was standing in a strange village with only one person left alive, on her way to other deserted and desolate villages.

The old man glared at her. All the same, his bitter eyes seemed to have softened a little as he stared at the dark-haired girl, who in turn looked pleadingly at him.

"Well, yes," he growled. "There was Wee Rasmus, of course. But there's not much room in his tumbledown little hovel. He was never a farmer, only a wretched landless peasant who helped the rest of us because he had nothing of his own."

Luke winked at Hanna. They both knew that farmers have a low opinion of those who own no land. But Luke reflected that surely it made no difference now, when they were all dead and buried.

"Can't you live in his house for the time being, perhaps," Luke wanted to say, "till the other farms are fit to live in again?" But then it occurred to him that it was probably no easier getting rid of ghosts on a farm than it was rats, and that was difficult enough. He reckoned that if only he guarded his words carefully enough, he could talk the old man around. Old people are often just the opposite of what you expect.

"Or perhaps you're afraid of meeting this Rasmus," he said, "in case he should come back all the same?" he added, as if casually.

"Wee Rasmus? Lord, no—I was never afraid of him in his lifetime, and I'm not going to start now!" The old man underlined his words with great sweeps of his arm.

"But perhaps his house is too far away?" continued Luke.

"No! It's there!" He raised a filthy hand and pointed toward a dismal little shack over by the churchyard wall.

"Well then, you'd do best to go there," said Hanna. She kept thinking how sad it was for the old man to have to live all by himself with the rats in the deserted village.

"It looks as if it's going to rain again," she continued. "We can't stay out here if it starts lightning and thundering again."

"I can't walk," said the old man in a pitiful voice—for he had become aware that somebody was feeling sorry for him. "My crutches were in there, and without my crutches I can only crawl. I had to crawl to get out, and even so the fire was singeing my behind."

"Never mind, we can help you," suggested Luke.

"Huh," he growled, "is that what you think? No, go into Piers's farm. There must be a pair of crutches somewhere in there, because Piers's son Peter used them during his last few years."

Luke went into Piers's farm without more ado. He found the crutches easily enough, and while he was at it, he took a few smoked sausages. It was good to have some food for when they continued their journey.

"How is it that you and the neighbor's son both had crutches?" he asked on his return.

"*Puh!*" the old man spat out. "It's all on account of Crutch-Olaf. He had a clubfoot and crutches," he added fiercely. "That was how he got the name."

The old man glanced hurriedly around to make sure that no living creature in the dead village should hear him. Then, to Luke's amazement, he sank his voice to a whisper.

"And *he*—Olaf—was a sorcerer! There's no doubt about it!"

"Where did Olaf live?" asked Luke.

"Shh!" The old man shut him up with a terrified air. "Olaf lived nowhere," he whispered. "He just turned up from time to time. He'd come limping first into one village, then into another. And you had to take care not to insult him by calling him Crutch-Olaf because then he might take a revenge that no human being can take unless the devil is helping him."

"How do you mean?" Now Luke, too, was whispering, gripped as he was by the strange, uncanny atmosphere.

The old man rolled his eyes wildly. "I mean Beelzebub and Satan and all the other dark ones from hell! He could call them up till the air seethed and crackled around him and stank of smoke and sulfur. That was what happened to Piers's Peter and to me—and to many others in these parts."

"Yes, but what did he do?" Hanna was so fascinated that she could not help interrupting.

The old man rolled his eyes still more wildly, and his single leg began to twitch. "You'll never believe it!" he said. "But Crutch-Olaf used to *say* something we couldn't make out, something terrible it must have been, and then he used to *point* at you and—*hey presto!*—your leg was gone, or your arm, or whatever he pointed at!"

Hanna and Luke listened to this incredible tale with open mouths. "The wh . . . wh . . . whole leg?" asked Luke in awestruck tones.

"Yes, that's to say, sometimes he would just point at the foot or a thumb or an ear. But whatever he pointed at, that was the end of that!"

"Did you see it happening?"

"Not always, of course, but we knew he did it. We knew it at once—when any of us lost anything! And once I did see it happening to a poor boy who'd been teasing him. 'Pst,' he said, and muttered something else, and then the whole boy was gone—vanished—gone to hell."

"Yes," said Luke, "but how did he do it?"

"Don't ask me," said the old man. "I'm no sorcerer."

The two children stood stock still in wonder.

"But now let's see what this fellow's crutches are like! Peter's—*ha-ha*—he's under the earth now—*ha-ha!*—deep down—as deep down as he deserves." The old man sat there grinning and mumbling away to himself.

"Give me a push now," he said suddenly, struggling to get up.

Luke pushed, and the old man got to his feet, trembling and lurching until he got his balance. Then he hobbled away on his crutches past the empty houses until he came to Wee Rasmus's wretched hut.

Hanna and Luke followed at a respectful distance. Hanna shook her head.

"He's gone mad—right out of his mind," she whispered. "Like that King of Babylon, the one who went on all fours and ate grass like a horse. It wouldn't surprise me if he started doing the same."

Luke nodded. "That's what comes of seeing too much."

"How do you mean?"

"Why, the plague and all the rest of it. And from being all alone. You start thinking there's somebody there to talk to or that they're coming—all those dark spirits he talked about."

Wee Rasmus's hut by the churchyard wall was easy to enter, for the door was unbarred. But the old man stood for a long time in the doorway, waving his arms, gesticulating, and mumbling in his beard. Finally he spat over his left shoulder three times, *puh, puh, puh,* said "Abracadabra," and then said the same word backward, "Arbadacarba."

"Why are you . . . ?" Hanna started to say.

"To get rid of the lot of them," hissed the old man. "Ghosts, evil thoughts, plague, everything. It's a good thing I've learned the words. How else do you think I'd have managed with all the evil spirits of the plague?"

Inside the hut there was only one room. A fireplace in the middle of the floor under the smoke hole and a heap of straw over by one wall were all it consisted of. Luckily there were no animals, neither dead domestic ones nor live rats. Up under the roof a ham and some sausages were still hanging.

"Could you live here?" asked Hanna. "If so, I expect we can find some things for you in the other farms."

"Yes," said the old man. "If you go to the third farm from here, that will be best. It's Simon's farm, and he was the only one who lived as well as I did."

And while they were helping to fetch fresh straw, blankets, and other necessities, they heard how the plague came to this village and how the rest of his household had left in the night.

"I heard them," he said. "They were creeping about and whispering, so that I shouldn't wake up. I could hear them packing food and turning the pigs and cows out since I couldn't look after them.

"But one of them stumbled over something in the dark with a great clatter. Till then I'd made up my mind to pretend I was asleep, but that clatter was more than I could have slept through. So I said in the dark, 'Shame on you—thieves and robbers—may you go to hell!'

"They fell silent. Then one of them—my daughter-in-law, Mia—said, 'There are no thieves and robbers here, Grandfather! There's only us!'

" 'Then what in heaven's name are you fumbling around for at this time of night?' I said. As if I didn't know perfectly well what they were up to. Nobody answered.

" 'Are you clearing out?' I asked. They still said nothing. I could hear them pottering around in the dark. They didn't know what to say; they had bad consciences.

"Finally Mia came and patted me all over, just as if I were a dog. 'You can't come with us, you know, Grandfather!' she said. Then her voice turned all sugary. 'But we'll be coming back when the plague is over—then we'll come home to you and everything.'

"My own wife said nothing. But I knew she was

there. A fine wife she was—she was as old as myself. But then she had the use of her two legs and everything else you need, so off she went.

"I thought they'd all gone, but then she came up to me and said sweetly, 'You see, you're no good at anything, Grandpa. But try now to manage for yourself until we come back. After all, we can't all stay here just for your sake. There's food in the house to last you a long time yet. What will happen when that's gone, the Lord must decide. And then we'll come back and meet again—if the plague hasn't taken us, or you, first.'

"But I got the better of her all the same," the old man went on with a grin. "As she was going out of the door, I pronounced a curse on her—a powerful secret curse that I'd learned from him—*puh!*—Crutch-Olaf. So that's cooked her goose.

"And now I'm certain she's dead," he continued, "because it's she who's sent the spirits from hell!"

Hanna shuddered at this ungodly talk. She only wished to get away, the sooner the better, but when the rain and thunder began again, they stayed.

It was late before they settled down to sleep. From time to time a streak of lightning flashed across the sky, lighting up the square smoke hole.

CHAPTER 7

The next morning the weather was again glorious. Birds sang from the heather-covered village roofs, and in the fields raindrops glittered like tiny sparks from a thousand blades of grass.

Luke stood outside Wee Rasmus's hut, drinking in the morning air, so beautifully fresh after the thunderstorm. Every now and then, however, there came a powerful, acrid breath from the scene of the fire.

He tiptoed into the hut and woke Hanna. At once she was wide awake, and joined him outside. "Let's be off," he whispered. She nodded, and a moment later they were on their way, satchels on their backs.

Luke thought his foot seemed better. He'd had a good rest, and the inflammation had gone down a little. But he still limped. "It's silly," he thought. "This may be the only long journey you'll ever make, and you have to hobble like an old nag!"

Leaving the village, they passed fields where only a little self-sown rye fought its way up through a thick carpet of weeds. When they reached the common on the outskirts, the children followed cart tracks that wound their way around bushes, small trees, and fresh puddles from the rain last night.

They had not gone far before Luke's foot began to hurt again, and progress became painfully slow. Luke walked with his eyes on the ground, taking great care how he placed his feet.

From time to time Hanna would begin to skip and dance. She had plenty of time while Luke was hobbling along, and the sunshine had put her in high spirits. "It's nice here," she said.

Luke went on hobbling and said nothing.

"All we need is a horse for you to ride," she continued.

Luke looked up. "Yes," he muttered, "that would certainly help."

"Well, isn't that extraordinary?" Hanna laughed and laughed, as if something was amusing her greatly.

"What?"

"Why, here we are, walking along, needing a horse more than anything else in the world—a small brown horse for you to ride . . ."

"There's nothing extraordinary in that," said Luke crossly.

"Take a look!" Hanna stopped beside him and pointed toward the bushes.

"Well, I never," said Luke.

"Now you can see for yourself." She laughed again.

In among the bushes was a small brown horse, wandering peacefully about, cropping the grass and nibbling at the bushes.

Luke blinked and rubbed his eyes several times. It was still there! "All the same, we'll never catch that horse," he muttered. "We may as well give up the idea. Horses are wild nowadays." And he resumed his hobbling.

Hanna pursed her lips and began to whistle—a long series of gentle little noises somewhere between a whistle and a cluck. The horse raised its head, looked in their direction, and neighed.

"Come here, horse!" called Hanna in her most enticing voice. And the horse actually came to her, neighing pleasantly, as if to say it had been looking forward to their arrival.

"It's obviously glad to meet people," said Hanna. As she approached the horse, she held out a piece of bread in her palm, and the horse ate it with great appetite.

Hanna patted the horse's neck and went on talking to it. The horse appeared to be enjoying the conversation. "Poor old thing," said Hanna. "It can hardly chew our dry bread."

"That I can well understand," said Luke. "I can hardly do so myself."

There was no need for a halter; the horse evidently liked being with the two wayfarers, and when they moved away, it followed at their heels.

Luke still went on hobbling, but from time to time he would look at the horse's head, which kept appearing over his shoulder, and wonder if it would work.

Hanna was asking herself the same question. "Don't you think you could treat yourself to a ride?" she asked finally. "You'd do much better, and I could easily keep up."

Luke stopped and patted the horse. Then he began talking to it, very calmly and seriously. "There now, old Crutch-Olaf," he said, for he kept remembering the old man's talk from last night. "There now, stand quite still." He patted the horse's neck and stroked its soft muzzle with one hand. "If old Crutch-Olaf will stand still, old Hobbling Luke can sit on you. I can't walk as well as you can because you're good at walking. Good, fast horse, let me sit on your back if you want to be a really kind horse . . ."

Hanna laughed and held the horse by the forelock while Luke mounted. "But you're riding a mare," she said, "so you mustn't call her Crutch-Olaf."

"What does it matter?" said Luke. "She may not even know that Crutch-Olaf is a boy's name, eh, old Crutch-Olaf?"

At all events, she seemed used to being ridden. Luke sat comfortably, for the horse had had plenty to eat and was as round as a barrel. He patted her neck. "Come on, then!" The horse ambled off at Hanna's heels.

"She may have been used as a saddle horse, by children perhaps," Luke remarked.

"Yes," said Hanna, wondering what had become of the last children who had ridden that horse. Had they left, or had the plague struck them? She wondered also what was happening at home. Claus Miller, too, had had a horse that the children were sometimes allowed to ride.

Soon they discovered that the horse could follow the road without help and there was no need for Hanna to lead the way. The horse just plodded straight ahead throughout the day. By evening they had covered as much ground as in the previous three or four days.

They spent the night under some bushes, with no covering but the clothes they slept in. The little mare grazed close at hand and was all ready to start the next morning.

Luke's foot soon improved with the rest, and by the third day he could walk without difficulty. After that they took turns in riding as they followed the winding cart tracks leading south over the flat plain toward Ribe. The landscape was distinctly bare and desolate, the villages being small, as well as few and far between, and the soil poor.

Only twice they met people. On one occasion they saw a young farmer and his wife and child, who were traveling north. The woman and the child were on horseback. They were some of the many people, perhaps, who had fled to avoid the plague.

"Look," said Hanna. "They're like the holy family that Master Jacob used to talk about."

Another time a pair of cattlemen approached from one side, driving a small herd of emaciated cattle. One of them shouted and beckoned to the children.

"What do you suppose they want?" asked Hanna, who was having her turn on the mare.

"I don't know, but we may as well hear what they have to say," Luke replied.

One of the cattlemen came on ahead of the other. He was short and stocky, and his hair and beard were so long that you could hardly see his face. "Could you give us a hand?" he called.

"Look out!" whispered Luke. "You'd better ride on ahead a bit—on horseback you can easily give him the slip."

"I can see he's got some kind of lasso, and I bet he means to use it." She urged the horse into a trot.

"What do you want a hand with?" shouted Luke.

When the cattleman saw Hanna riding away, he made no effort to conceal his fury. "Come back!" he bawled.

By now Luke had heard enough, and he broke into a run. The cattleman started running, too, but soon gave up the pursuit as he found himself falling farther and farther behind.

"What a pair!" Luke gasped when he had caught up with Hanna. "They were after the horse. I'm sure they found those animals around here—the dead villages are full of them."

"I thought it was me they were after," said Hanna. "In any case, it's a good thing we got away safely."

"Don't you think the plague must be nearly over," she continued a moment later, "when people are starting to go home?"

"Oh, if only it is," Luke said with a sigh.

But the villages they passed through continued to be deserted.

Gradually the two children came to know each other better and better. They had plenty of time on the road for telling each other about their lives in the days before the plague. When they talked about it, they could hardly understand that only a year ago those had been their ordinary, daily lives.

Luke had been at home with his parents and brothers and sisters in Ullsthorp, looking after the sheep with his younger brother Simon. The youngest in a family always began with the sheep; then as he grew older and more experienced, he was promoted to tending the cattle. Hanna had been a farm girl at Claus Miller's in Finthorp.

Hanna continued to brood on all the things Grandma Miller had spoken of. "Grandma Miller was right," she said to Luke. "The country was to be emptied of people—and here we are traveling through an uninhabited land. The terrible plague has been." In addition, so many of the old woman's other prophecies were being fulfilled: she had already met somebody her own age and had set out on a long and difficult journey.

That evening they came to a deep, wide stream. Here the road divided. Some of the cart tracks seemed to continue straight into the water, while others followed the river east. They had not seen such a river since the time Jacob had helped them on their way, but they remembered all too vividly what it was like when in midcurrent it seemed as if at any moment the water might come over their heads. They were a little nervous about wading into a river they knew nothing about—except what they could see.

They had thought Crutch-Olaf would help when it came to crossing a river, but they had to think again. The little mare was ready enough to go down to the water's edge and slake her thirst, but that was all. Neither threats nor cajolements could make her take one single step into the water.

So Luke himself had a go, but after a few steps he could feel the bottom falling steeply away, and he came uncomfortably close to being swept off his feet by the current.

Back on dry land, he wrung the water out of his clothes and hung them on the bushes to dry, while he lay on the soft grass. "We'll have to follow the river," he said. "Maybe we'll find a better place to cross. In any case, it's no good here."

A little later they set out east along the riverbank. Both were beginning to weary of the long journey. All those hot, strenuous days and the tension whenever they met somebody or came to a village had taken their toll. Gradually they had come to long for somebody else to talk to.

Toward sunset they came to a thicket, where they decided to camp for the night. They had eaten a little of their dry, hard bread, and now they were lying and resting. They had little to say to each other, for they were tired and sleepy.

Suddenly Luke sat up and turned his head toward the road they had left. "There are some people coming," he whispered.

Hanna was lying curled up in the grass, her bag under her head. "It's all right—they can't see us," she murmured sleepily, but Luke rose cautiously and peered over the bushes.

"Well, I never," he said in a low voice, continuing to stare as Hanna joined him.

On the road along which they themselves had traveled came a whole crowd of people. They could see only their heads, which seemed to hover above the bushes. It was impossible to count them exactly, but there must have been twenty or thirty of them, both men and women.

The two children looked at the group with mingled amazement and terror. They had been on their own so long that they could do with some company, but they had grown wary of strangers—you never knew whether you could trust them or what sort of people they were.

"Shall we . . . ?" Hanna started to say. But she didn't complete the sentence; she was still of two minds. Dare they really approach a crowd of complete strangers?

Luke lay down again. "We'll stay here for tonight. Tomorrow morning . . . we'll see."

The strangers evidently had the same idea as the children: it was evening and time to pitch some sort of camp.

A continuous background of voices and sounds from their encampment prevented Hanna and Luke from sleeping. Later in the evening they could see smoke and flames a little farther along the road. At least they were people who needed to eat, rest, and sleep, yet it was a long time before they became quiet.

"Do you think they're robbers?" asked Hanna.

Luke shook his head. "You shouldn't think the worst about people," he said, "—at least, not always—or the best either, but something in between. Perhaps they're refugees like us. And perhaps," he continued, "if we keep our ears open, we'll learn what sort of people they are."

Only it was difficult to decide, not because of the distance, which was hardly more than a few hundred yards, nor because of any lack of sounds—it was easy to hear what was going on. There were shouts, talk, bickering, snatches of song, the chopping of wood. But later, when it was almost dark, they could see the campfires and hear that the entire group was singing hymns, one after another, with husky men's voices and shrill women's ones.

And at intervals they heard a single powerful voice praying or intoning.

What on earth did it mean? Prayers and hymns in the still summer night? It was certainly something out of the usual.

"In any case, I don't think they're robbers," said Hanna. "Do you think robbers sit around their campfires singing hymns?"

"No," said Luke. "People would always hear them and be on their guard."

When Hanna said her prayers that night, she felt rather more secure than she had for a long time. Luke lay at her side, while from the encampment the singing continued loud and clear. In the thicket behind them Crutch-Olaf was cropping the grass. She felt they were no longer alone.

CHAPTER 8

The next morning the countryside was veiled in mist. On every side there was nothing but gray; even the bushes were swallowed up in the gray. From the strangers' encampment the children could hear shouting and talking in the still morning air.

"We must find a way of getting around them," said Luke. He had no inclination to go too close to the strangers. One never knew what sort of people they were. "I think we should push on and try to cross that river somewhere or other," he continued.

Hanna nodded. "It's a long time since we've spoken to other people," she said. "Do you think they're dangerous?"

"Dangerous . . . dangerous," muttered Luke. "I don't know what they are. I only know I'm not going near people who sit singing hymns half the night!"

"For goodness' sake, what does that matter? At least we'd have somebody to ask for the way once in a while." Hanna was just a tiny bit disappointed.

But soon afterward they were on their way.

They had to make a tiresome detour through a dense oak thicket in order to avoid both the camp and a thick patch of brambles. Eventually they rejoined the river—and the cart tracks, which continued along the riverbank.

All that day and the next they followed the windings of the river, even though they began to suspect they were on the wrong road. The river was still too wide and deep for them to venture across, but it was getting perceptibly narrower the farther east they went.

The journey was mostly monotonous until they suddenly came upon a village right beside the river and the road. To their astonishment, outside of one of the gray farms stood a bearded peasant and a woman.

From the road the children made out a ladder leaning against the wall, and from the ladder hung a newly slaughtered pig. Ladder and paving stones alike were red with blood, which a striped cat was calmly licking up. The man was using a heavy ax to cut the pig in two from end to end, from its snout to its tail. His bare torso gleamed with sweat in the hot sun.

Hanna and Luke came a little nearer and stood watching the peasant couple. Crutch-Olaf wandered along the riverbank savouring the lush grass.

"Shall we ask them?" Luke whispered. He felt safer with village people. He knew what they were like.

Hanna nodded eagerly, but Luke preferred to wait until the man had finished his chopping operations—neither he nor the woman had noticed their two visitors. The woman at once started removing the entrails with a long knife.

Luke was on the point of stepping forward and speaking when something happened that stopped him dead. From the barn emerged two children—two emaciated-looking boys of five or six, ragged, barefoot, and gray with dirt.

"We *must* keep them," said the woman, without pausing in her work with the knife. "The poor mites have nowhere else to go."

"But supposing," said the man, "some of their own people are still alive? After all, we don't know how many the plague has carried off." He crossed himself with two bloodstained fingers. "It may have spared some of them."

"Look," retorted the woman, "we don't even know where they come from or what their names are. How are we going to find out if any of their people are still alive?"

"If only they'd been a bit bigger," grumbled the man, "they might have done something to earn their keep."

"Never mind about that," said the woman firmly. "We can't let an innocent pair of children like that run wild in the forest—they'd die of hunger as soon as winter came. They *must* stay here; there are no two ways about it." As if to underline her words, she flung down a whole handful of pig's entrails with such violence that they hit the paving stones with a loud smack.

"All right, all right," said the man good-humoredly. "Let them stay here since there's no alternative."

"There'd never have been so much argy-bargy with my poor Peter," said the woman bitterly. "And if you're going to stay here in my farm, you'd better learn to do as I say and not be so pigheaded about everything."

The man wiped the sweat off his forehead with the

back of his hand and waved a cloud of flies away. Then, leaning quietly on his enormous ax and grinning to himself, he called out to the two boys, who all this time had been standing hand in hand by the door, "Well, come on then!"

The boys continued to stand there. The younger put a finger in his mouth; the elder held the younger's hand a little tighter.

"Come on then, come on then!" said the man, tapping his knee—the way you do when calling to a puppy.

"Can't you see they're frightened? Give them some bread," said the woman. She spread her elbows and inspected herself. "There's as much blood on me as there is in the pig!"

The man put down the ax and disappeared. A moment later he returned with a piece of bread and a stump of sausage. Going up to the boys, he held the food in front of them. Hanna noticed how they devoured it with their eyes. Suddenly the older boy made a rush at the food and snatched it from the man's hand; then he rushed back again.

The boys began to eat, greedily and ravenously, without chewing properly—and the mouthfuls were much too big, thought Hanna. She knew they must be hungry to eat like that. They stayed over by the barn door, and at each mouthful they looked warily at the peasant couple—ready to bolt if necessary. "They must be famished," Hanna said to herself. "What a blessing they can eat at last!"

"Well," said the peasant, "I'd better go and see if I can find those cows again." As he turned to go, his eye fell on Luke and Hanna. "Hello, hello," he said, "here's two more!" He raised his voice. "Are you hungry, too?"

They realized they had been standing and staring at the two small boys. Luke went up to the man; Hanna followed a pace or two behind.

"No-o," said Luke, "we were just passing, and . . . and . . . we were going to ask . . ."

The woman interrupted. "Of course you're hungry—everyone's hungry nowadays, and as long as I've food in the house, I'll give some to anyone who's hungry—anyone who comes here and needs it. I know for myself what it's like. Come and eat!"

"That wasn't why we came!" Hanna, who had taken an immediate liking to the brisk woman, felt it was her turn to say something. "It's just that we can't find a place to cross the river."

"All right, we can talk about that afterwards," the woman answered. "What's more, if you'll give me a hand with the work here, you can take some food with you—if you're going farther. You"—speaking to Luke—"can go and look for the cows with Matthew, and you"—turning to Hanna—"can help me get this meat into the salting tub."

Luke and Hanna exchanged a quick glance, their eyes asking, "Shall we?" Luke nodded.

Presently Luke went off with the peasant, and Hanna helped the woman to cut up the pig and put the pieces in the salting tub.

It was almost like old times, and she kept thinking of the slaughtering season back at Claus Miller's. As they worked, she learned many things. The woman was clearly glad to have Hanna's help, but she was almost equally glad to have somebody to talk to, or at least somebody who would listen to her.

At the moment they were the only people in this village, but others would probably be returning, like the two on this farm; for both Matthew and the woman, whose name was Marta, were locals. They had hidden in the woods to escape the plague, whose victims included her husband and Matthew's wife.

"Matthew and I have been neighbors for many years," said Marta. "I know him like the back of my hand. He's not nearly as bright as my poor Peter was, but at least he's better than nothing." She sighed. "How is a poor woman to manage a farm all on her own?"

Hanna learned from Marta what it had been like to spend days and nights on end alone in the forest, and the horror of coming home to a dead, desolate village. But then, fortunately, Matthew had turned up, and now they were busy laying in supplies. They had even managed to catch some of the piebald pigs that had taken to the forest.

Last night the two small boys had arrived in the village. They did not live here—they had just come wandering into the village over the fields—and they had been so frightened that they refused to come into the house, preferring to sit out in the barn.

Now they were sitting in the farmyard, rooting around in the earth. Hanna could see that they had started to play. One was digging with his hands in the cracks between the flagstones, and the other was beating the earth with a stone. The striped cat came inquisitively up to them and began rubbing itself against their legs. They were so absorbed by the cat and by what they were doing that they took no notice whatever of Hanna, who came quietly up to them, squatted on her haunches, and began talking to the cat. "Puss, puss, puss!"

She would have liked to talk to the boys, but they were still too frightened. She needed to go very carefully.

"Puss, puss," she said, stroking the cat. "This *is* a nice place you've come to, little puss! This is Hanna stroking you—and indoors Marta is making food for us all. And Matthew is out finding a cow to give you some milk. And down by the river there's a little brown horse called Crutch-Olaf—and here are two boys who want to play with you."

All the time Hanna spoke only to the cat, as if the boys didn't exist. When she stopped speaking, they both sat looking at her with large eyes and open mouths.

"And what do you think their names are? Do you know, little puss?" She stroked the cat again, and it settled itself in her lap, purring contentedly. She sat like that for a long time, talking on and on, until suddenly the younger boy said, "Where'sh horsh?"

He didn't speak to anybody in particular, but just to the world at large.

"Gone!" answered the older boy.

"Where'sh horsh?" the boy repeated.

Hanna understood, or thought she did. "You mean the horse?" she said. "Can you say horse? Not horsh—horse."

He looked at her and gave a single quick nod. For a moment it seemed to Hanna as if he were about to smile.

"Shall we go and find the horse?" she asked.

He nodded again.

"Come!" Hanna got up. "Come with Hanna and we'll

find the horse." She stretched out her hand to the boy. He got up, but kept both hands behind his back. The older boy, too, got up. "Come!" she repeated as she set off past the dunghill and down to the river. The boys followed at a suitable distance.

"There's Crutch-Olaf!" she said when they had passed the houses. She pointed at the horse, who was ambling around a little way off. Then she gave a gentle little whistle, which the horse immediately recognized. Crutch-Olaf lifted her head, neighed, and started coming toward them. Hanna patted the horse and gathered her forelock into a point so that it wouldn't hang down over the animal's eyes.

The boys still stayed at a safe distance.

"If only they weren't so frightened," thought Hanna. But perhaps they would pluck up courage to pat the horse when they saw that nothing happened when she did so.

Then she had an idea: with a swift movement she sprang up on the horse's back. The horse thought they were on their way and started to walk.

"Woa!" she said, and the horse stopped. Hanna sat there for a little before dismounting again. "Do you want to try?" she said to the younger boy.

It wasn't as easy as that, however. The two needed a lot of talk and persuasion before they would even pat the horse. But Hanna persisted, and finally she even succeeded in getting them up on the horse's back.

It was a long time, though, before she could get them to talk. Crutch-Olaf had begun grazing again, and Hanna was on the way back to the farm with the two boys. "Phew!" she exclaimed with a laugh as she stretched herself out in the long grass between the houses.

The boys stood gazing at her.

"My word, I'm tired," she said, breathing heavily. "Aren't you tired, too?"

"Yes, tired!" said the younger boy, and he stretched himself out with his arms under his head like Hanna. The older boy sat down and began plucking some white flowers.

"What's your name?" asked Hanna. It was the first time she had asked the question directly.

The boy wriggled a little, but presently the answer came: "Pip!"

"I'm Hanna." She pointed at herself. "Hanna!" she said again. Then she pointed at him and said, "Pip!" She repeated the pantomime half a dozen times.

The boy gazed at her for a long time; then he smiled —or so it seemed to Hanna—and pointed, first at himself and then at Hanna, saying, "Pip—Hanna—Pip—Hanna—Pip—Hanna." Then he gave a loud laugh.

Hanna was delighted. She laughed and repeated the names several times more. The older boy joined in the laughter.

"What's your name?" she asked.

The boy sat tearing up a daisy, which he'd picked. "Jack," he whispered. And to demonstrate his knowledge, he pointed and said, "Jack—Pip—Hanna!" Then they all had a good laugh; but suddenly Jack said, "I'm hungry!"

"Pip hungry, too!"

"You're going to eat now!" Hanna was glad that she had managed to make them talk, but all the time she had been thinking to herself that they badly needed a wash.

Their legs were the same color as the earth, their arms were streaked black and gray, and their faces were smeared all over with mud and dirt. Their hair was caked in grime and stuck out in all directions. But how to get them clean?

"Come!" she said, jumping to her feet. The boys followed her readily enough down to the river. Having made sure that it was not too deep near the bank, she rapidly took off her clothes and went into the water. Here she jumped around and splashed herself vigorously, laughing to show what fun it all was. Finally she took a tuft of grass and rubbed herself all over. This was probably the best way to get the boys into the water. They watched her for a bit; then she helped them out of their ragged clothes and into the water.

When they returned to the village, the boys were barely recognizable. They were clean again! All they needed was some better clothes, and Hanna trusted that one day they would get them.

The woman was engaged in roasting a large chunk of the newly slaughtered pig. She had stuck it on the end of a long spit, which from time to time she turned on its stand. It smelled good, and they were allowed to taste a morsel with some hard bread.

Hanna helped Marta again with the housework and then with chores out in the barn. There were only a few animals, but those that were there needed tending. A black-and-white pig lay in one corner of the dark barn. At first Hanna could see nothing; she could only hear something there. When she approached, she made out a sow and a litter of piglets—seven as far as she could count. Outside, a number of rough-haired, skinny pigs were rooting around the remains of their slaughtered companion. To Hanna's amazement they were eating with a hearty appetite.

On the threshing floor there was still a little unthreshed corn. Hanna sniffed. There was a strong smell of mice, as in every village they had passed through, so it was unlikely to be worth bothering with these remnants, she thought, for she had seen before how mice can ruin corn. There must have been scores of them here because the striped cat, which had followed her in, idled around like a cat that has had a surfeit of mice and lost all interest in them.

Toward evening Matthew and Luke returned. They had caught only a few aged cows and a heifer. But they said there were many more creatures in the forest, only so wild that it had been difficult to get near them—especially as Luke's foot was again sore and swollen and he could not run properly.

It seemed strange to be sitting down to a meal around a table; it reminded Luke of his home at Ullsthorp. Pleasantly tired after the day's work, they all sat eating together—Hanna and Luke, the two boys, Matthew and Marta. It was almost as if they were a family, and yet none of them were related; they had merely been blown together by a strong wind—the plague.

Suddenly Hanna thought she could hear something. At first she persuaded herself that the sound came from inside her own head, from her chewing, but gradually she became certain that it came from outside. She could not quite place the noise, which was almost like the thump you hear if you put your ear to a cow's belly. For a long time she listened to the thumping and forgot to eat.

She looked at the others. Their jaws had stopped moving, and they were all sitting with baited breath, listening with all their concentration. They exchanged glances, but nobody spoke.

Now there was a second sound in addition to the thumping: the sound of a flute, and then singing.

Matthew put his great hands on the edge of the table and rose heavily to his feet. "We'd better . . ." he said as he moved toward the door. As he went, he picked up his ax. They all stared at it—it was still red with blood from the slaughter. The others got up and followed, their hearts beating at the double from fear.

"It's drums," whispered Marta, who was visibly frightened. "Drums and flutes." She had lived longer than the children and knew that drums usually meant soldiers —and soldiers meant trouble: war, plunder, fire, and the sword.

"Haven't we suffered enough with the plague?" she whispered. "Heaven help us!"

They hid in the barn, determined that nobody should find them. Marta glanced up at the smoke hole before going into the mud-built barn; fortunately there was no smoke to betray their presence.

They stood looking out through the numerous cracks in the mud walls of the barn. Hanna and Luke each stood at a separate chink. Nobody said a word—they just gazed and gazed at the extraordinary procession advancing along the road beside the river.

First came a number of men carrying flags on long poles. One flag was white with a red cross; a second consisted of a huge green eye with long lines radiating from it like the rays of the sun; a third had a picture of a man in armor, with a great sword in his hand and long shafts of light around his face.

"That's . . . that must be Saint Michael," whispered Hanna, "the one with the sword, don't you think?"

Luke said nothing in reply. He hardly knew what he thought, and indeed he had not heard what Hanna said, being too intent on watching the next group: a number of gaudily dressed men with drums, which they were beating in a rapid rhythm. Their unkempt hair and beards fluttered in the wind.

Next came a pair of short-bearded men playing a mournful tune on the flute. Behind them came a throng of men and women carrying various things on their backs: leather bags, rugs, long staves. A short distance behind the rest came two men pulling a two-wheeled cart. As they came past the barn, they started to sing.

"It must be the same people who sang that night we slept in the thicket," said Luke. "Don't you recognize the tune?"

Hanna nodded. "But who are they?" she asked.

Luke shrugged his shoulders. "I don't think they can be soldiers or anything like that—they've no weapons—no spears or swords."

Matthew said, "I think they're people who go about whipping themselves. They say there are quite a few of them about these days. Flagellants, I believe they're called."

"What do they do that for?" Luke wanted to know.

"I don't really know," answered Matthew, "but I met a mendicant friar in the forest, and he told me about them. It seems they ask God to forgive their own and other people's sins to make the plague come to an end.

According to him, the reason why they flog themselves is to show how much they regret their sins. They think God won't need to punish us so severely—with the plague and other misfortunes—if they give a helping hand with the punishing.

"I can't rightly make it out," Matthew added by and by. "Because it isn't only the rogues who die of the plague; it's good honest folks as well—and some of us who survived weren't as good as we should have been. No, I don't understand that sort of thing." Matthew shook his head.

"It's time we went in and got some sleep," said Marta, when it was almost dark. "There's plenty to do tomorrow and for many a day ahead. If we're going to be the only people in this village"—she sighed—"there's a number of things we shall have to see to—that is, if we don't want to go hungry this winter."

"We have to go to Ribe," said Luke, "and that's a long way."

"Yes," said Matthew, "it certainly is. You'll be tired by the time you get there!"

"You can stay here," said Marta quietly. "You'll be all right here."

Neither Hanna nor Luke answered. They were thinking about the long journey they had set out on.

After they settled down for the night, they did not sleep at once. For a time they talked about those strange men and women called flagellants. And they talked about the journey to Ribe.

Marta lay in the usual housewife's place near the hearth so that she could look after the fire, and the two small boys were next to her. Matthew lay in the head of the family's place, nearest the door. He had his great ax by his side, within easy reach.

Hanna looked around her in the darkened room, thinking how nice it was to spend a night under a roof. She noticed a whole row of sleeping places along the length of one wall. Just ordinary sleeping places they were—a low platform of turf with a good layer of hay on top.

"There've been a lot of people living here," she said, but nobody answered her, and presently she could hear Marta weeping.

Before long Matthew began snoring—a peaceful, soporific sound. Shortly afterward Hanna could tell that Luke, too, had fallen asleep. For a moment she had the feeling that everything was well. The peaceful sounds of breathing made it easy to forget all the horrors.

Then she was wide awake again. She had the impression that a long time had passed, though she could still hear Marta crying—almost silently, but there was no mistaking the way she was breathing. Hanna regretted her remark about many people having lived in the house, which was of course Marta's house. Marta had probably had children. She had said nothing about them, but Hanna was certain she had had children who had died from the plague.

For a long time she listened to Marta's quiet weeping. How could she comfort her?

Suddenly Hanna heard rustling noises from the direction of the two boys. Then the younger one began whimpering and talking in his sleep. This went on for quite a while. Then he got up, and his bare feet pattered across the hard mud floor. He was wandering around as if he were searching for something.

"He needs to go out," Hanna thought. "Perhaps I ought to get up and help him find the door." Then it was too late. He must have given up trying to find the door in the dark, and he was standing over in the corner. Hanna could hear a thin trickling sound in the silent house.

Marta heard it, too. She sat up, and Hanna heard her whisper, "Come, little boy," as the feet came pattering back.

The little fellow went across to Marta and lay down beside her with a peaceful, contented sigh. Marta stopped crying.

CHAPTER 9

A little way off a cock crowed. Luke heard it, clear and distinct. The cock came nearer and nearer until it shrilled in his ears, and he woke up.

The cock was sitting up on the beam under the roof —a big, speckled bird that sat there looking around him with an air of importance. Luke had not noticed him last night; he must have been sitting there quite silently until now, when it was daybreak.

Luke crawled out from under the hay and peered out of the door at the village. It was early morning. A blackbird with a yellow beak was sitting up on one of the roofs, fluting away. Surely it was late in the season for a bird to be singing such a song. Autumn would soon be here, but perhaps it had only just finished building its nest, long after all the others. At the dung heap the rats were fighting for the last remnants of yesterday's pig; otherwise, all was still. The sun was hidden by the white mist that still lay over the meadows and the village. Luke sat down on a heap of sticks by the fireplace. Today they were to continue on their journey! It cheered him to know that they were on their way and that soon they would be crossing the river. Good! If only the others would wake up soon.

Luke deliberately kept his thoughts on the journey and all the new sights and experiences they could expect. He was determined not to think about his foot because it was hurting so badly—much worse than yesterday.

He looked around him at the sleepers. Matthew was lying on his back, mouth agape. His brown beard trembled each time he breathed, and a gentle snoring came from his direction. The younger boy, Pip, was lying with one thin arm around Marta's brown neck, and both of them were sleeping peacefully. Marta's long hair was hanging down over the boy, almost hiding his face.

"Lucky fellow," thought Luke. He was reminded of his younger brothers.

Jack's place was empty! Where could he be? Then Luke had to laugh. The boy was lying rolled up like a cat, with his head against Hanna's back.

Were the two boys brothers? Or had they merely chanced to meet somewhere or other? They themselves were unable to say. Luke thought how strange it would be for them as they grew older. Perhaps they would not know who they were, what their real names were, or who their parents were—and nobody else could tell them. They were lucky to have found a place to live; they would certainly thrive under Marta's and Matthew's care.

Luke took a little tour of the village's farms. There was little to see, and that little was the same as in other places. Houses stood gaping with empty doors and gates; in the farmyards weeds were shooting up between the paving stones, and between the houses there was a strong smell of camomile flowers, which stretched all the way down to the river.

As soon as he heard signs of life, he turned back into the house. The others were all up now.

A little later, as they sat eating the hard black bread and drinking a little fresh milk, Luke told about his Uncle Nicholas in Ribe and a little about what had happened to them all at home.

Matthew simply nodded and told them once more how to cross the river. It was not far to the ford by the burial mounds, and it was easy to find.

But Marta said, "Why don't you stay here? You'll be better off with us than traveling all that distance. We can do with your help, and you're strong and able to do your full share of the work."

"They don't believe we'll ever find Uncle Nicholas," thought Luke.

Matthew sat running his forefinger through his beard. "Yes," he said, "we need every hand that can work —and it's lucky there are two hands to every mouth since the two little fellows can't do much to help. You can certainly stay here if you want to."

At this moment Jack and Pip came running in. Nobody had noticed them going out, but now here they were rushing in at the door and talking one against the other.

It was Hanna they wanted to tell something to, but it was beyond her powers to understand them since they were both talking at the same time. She laughed at their eagerness and tried to shut Pip up so that she could hear what Jack had to say.

"What did you say? It's gone?"

"Yes, gone away," said the boy.

"Are you certain?"

The boy nodded. "It's gone away!"

Luke suddenly pricked up his ears. "Who's gone away?" he asked uneasily.

"Crutch-Olaf! She's gone!"

"She's probably just hiding somewhere," he said lightly. He hadn't even thought of the horse when he was out just now. She had been left entirely to her own devices since last night.

"Let's look in the houses," said Matthew. "There are so many empty stables, and she probably wanted to be indoors. I expect she's been used to a stable before. We could go all around the village looking for her."

"If only it isn't . . . them," whispered Hanna, "the people last night." As she spoke, she clapped her hand to her mouth—but she had said it.

Luke said nothing, but he began to be afraid she was right. However, they made a rapid search through every empty house and farm in the village. The search was soon over, for the village was not very big. The horse was nowhere to be found!

"It's bound to be them who took her," said Hanna when they were back at Marta's farm.

"I never gave Crutch-Olaf a thought," said Luke. "Last night, I mean. She must have been right in their path, and they could certainly do with a horse to pull their baggage."

"We'll chase after them," said Hanna. She was so angry and upset that she was almost in tears.

"Yes," muttered Luke, "we'll certainly do that. This

confounded foot! If only it wasn't so painful, I'd soon catch up with them."

Once again, well stocked with food, they were on the road. Matthew and Marta would gladly have kept them, and when the younger of the two small boys would not let go of Hanna, it occurred to her that if they failed to find Uncle Nicholas, they could always come back here.

Their journey, however, had become more complicated than before because they had first to look for Crutch-Olaf before continuing on their way to Ribe.

"If it's the flogging folk who've taken the horse," Matthew had said, "you'd better not waste more time on them because you won't get it back in any case!"

Their progress seemed terribly slow to Luke with his swollen foot. Hanna comforted him as best she could.

Toward midday a violent storm blew up. With no houses or trees nearby, Luke and Hanna were obliged to seek shelter under a thick bush, yet even here they were soon soaked to the skin by the violent rain.

When the storm was over, they continued once more along the riverbank.

"I don't think that river's going to be easy to cross," said Hanna. "It seems to me there's more water in it than there was before."

"Of course," Luke answered irritably. "All that rain has to go somewhere, and that somewhere is the river!" He was tired, wet, and miserable. The pain from his swollen foot was spreading, making his whole leg throb and ache right up to the groin. The sweat poured off him, and his head swam.

It was almost evening before they reached the ford by the burial mounds. Although they could still see tracks leading down to the water, it was obvious that they would not be able to cross the river with all the water that was in it now.

"Look!" Hanna suddenly shouted, pointing across the river. "There—there's Crutch-Olaf!"

Luke followed her finger with his eye. There on the other side the entire band of flagellants was camped on a little hill. They must have crossed by the ford before the storm, and now they were resting after their exertions. And, sure enough, the little brown horse was grazing contentedly at the edge of the group.

"Yes," he said, "that's her all right!"

"Just you wait!" Hanna muttered threateningly, her fists clenched. "You pack of thieves!"

"Yes, wait," growled Luke. "We've no choice but to wait—first for the water to go down and then for me to hobble after them!"

"You damned pack of thieves!" said Hanna, but she was no longer quite so angry. It didn't help in any case.

"This accursed foot," said Luke.

Hanna said, hoping to console him a little, "Yes, it is a curse, but let's be thankful that you haven't lost it altogether!"

And so they waited.

The next morning there was as much water in the river as ever. They could only stay where they were, watching helplessly as the entire band struck camp and disappeared into the hills—flags, drums, flutes, and—right at the back—Crutch-Olaf pulling a little cart!

All that day they sat and waited. Luke lay drowsing most of the time, while Hanna wandered around inspecting the countryside.

By evening the water was perceptibly lower, and the next morning they were able to cross. This time they knew how to keep their clothes dry by carrying them in bundles on their heads. If only the water was not too deep! They just managed as the water came up to their chins.

Luke's foot was in such a state that he had to go more slowly than ever. The chances of their overtaking the gang seemed remote, but at least they had their tracks to follow—including Crutch-Olaf's.

So it went for several days until one fine morning they came to a town. Hanna had gone on ahead through the forest of young trees they had been crossing. Suddenly she stopped dead and waited until Luke caught up with her. She said nothing, but simply pointed.

Luke said nothing either, for he shared her feelings. Neither of them had ever seen a town before!

Ahead of them lay a green valley. But at the foot of the valley, between the surrounding hills, lay what could only be a town. There were gray roofs made of straw and in between a few red roofs of some other material. In the middle of the town was a larger building with a great red tower reaching up into the sky, but the most wonderful thing of all was the water. Beyond the town lay a broad, calm streak of water that stretched as far as the eye could see.

Eventually Hanna whispered, "Don't you think that must be . . . the sea?"

They had both heard of the great stretch of water

known as the sea, but this was quite different from what they had imagined.

"I thought it would look soft," said Luke, "not hard like iron."

"Isn't it huge!" whispered Hanna, still completely fascinated.

Presently they continued on their way toward the town, which drew them like a magnet with all its strange new sights. Much later they remembered with surprise that they had not been frightened. At the time it never occurred to them. All they thought of was Crutch-Olaf and the mass of exciting new impressions.

All around the town was a high palisade of long stakes. But straight ahead lay a gate—the largest gate they had ever seen. Through it crowds of people hurried in and out. Some carried objects in their hands or on their backs: baskets, sticks, cloth, or a slaughtered pig. Others were followed by cattle coming in from the fields, while still others drove herds of pigs.

Never had they met with such a hubbub as when they passed through the gate into the city—people shouting and scolding, dogs barking, hens screeching, geese cackling, and a piebald pig squealing in wild terror as somebody thrashed it without mercy. And on either side of the street were houses that echoed the tumult.

Hanna held her nose as she walked. The din she could bear, but not the stench from the filth that lay around wherever they went and in which the animals were constantly rooting around. In the sweltering heat the smell was almost unbearable. A large cock started to crow and flap its wings, stirring up a cloud of dust that made Hanna sneeze.

Luke was so giddy that he had almost ceased to notice his surroundings. His foot tortured him, the sweat poured off him, and he was on the point of vomiting.

Once, when he looked up at the houses, he was surprised to find them swaying to and fro, like trees in a gale. He closed his eyes, but when he opened them again, the houses had started to dance. After that he kept his eyes firmly on the ground.

"Let's get out of this!" he said with a groan. The dust was choking him so that he could hardly speak. "Let's get out of this town—out into the forest."

Hanna looked at him as if unable to understand his words, but there was no time to get away, and no room.

Suddenly they heard a familiar sound—yes, drums! —drums and flutes. And another sound that pierced through the rest. They found themselves compelled to hold on to each other for dear life as people pushed madly on every side—so many that the mere sight was dizzying. Everybody wanted to see what was going on.

It was the flogging folk—flagellants as Matthew had called them. As the band approached the gate, people made way for them, and the children managed to see them—flags, drums, flutes, and all.

At first Luke could not make out what the noise was that he heard above the thump of the drums and the piping of the flutes—it sounded like shouts and screams, but screams such as he had never heard before. Was this what people were like in a town, that they shouted and screamed so wildly?

Hanna's stomach was turned almost inside out—for now she could see it all. She closed her eyes.

The flagellants had stripped to the waist and were

lashing themselves with long cords or whips. Hanna could see their backs laced with blood even with her eyes closed, and all the time the shouts and screams re-echoed through the streets.

It was so strange and hideous that Hanna burst into tears, clasping Luke's hand so tightly that he winced with pain.

Luke, too, had seen the gang as it whirled around him faster and faster, and despite the pain, he was glad to feel Hanna's hand. The earth swayed beneath him; he held on to Hanna as best he could.

"I'm ill," he kept saying to himself. "Hold on tight or you'll go under."

Suddenly Hanna gave a start. There she was! *The horse!*

Calmly and unconcernedly Crutch-Olaf was pulling a little two-wheeled cart, quite indifferent to the wild goings-on around her.

If only there weren't so many people in the street! It was almost impossible to move.

But Hanna was determined, absolutely determined, to get to the horse. She ducked under arms, made detours around people, in and out, getting steadily nearer and nearer to the horse. Finally she stretched out her hand and touched it.

"Crutch-Olaf!" she shouted. "Stop—wait—whoa—stay here!"

CHAPTER 10

The first thing that Luke became aware of was a sheepskin. It was tickling his nose, and it smelled of sheep.

Next, he discovered that he was lying on his back, looking up at something he did not recognize. Not trees or bushes, nor the sky, nor an ordinary ceiling, but something different! He turned his head to one side and saw a gray mud wall. Then he turned to the other side, slowly and with difficulty. He felt as if there were a stone or some other heavy object tied to his head. On the floor at his side sat a girl. She had fair hair and was perhaps a little younger than he.

"I'm in a house," he thought. "How can that have happened?"

The girl sat quite still, looking down at him. His movement must have attracted her attention.

Luke closed his eyes, then opened them again a fraction. He could see through his eyelashes that the girl was wearing a green dress. She had raised herself onto her knees and was bending over him with an inquiring air. When he opened his eyes fully, she continued to look at him without embarrassment, gazing into his eyes unblinkingly. Her own were as blue as the sky in summer.

His throat was sore. Perhaps it would help if he drank something. He wanted to tell the girl he was thirsty, but when he tried to speak, he could only move his lips and produce a sound resembling a snarl.

The girl doubtless thought the strange boy was showing his teeth and snarling at her. At all events, she got up quickly and went away. Luke was unable to see where she went.

He lay there looking around the room. There were boards above the beams, so that he was unable to see the roof, but in the gaps between the boards hung a little hay. Immediately above him was a hole in the wall, with a shutter that stood ajar. Through this hole light poured into the room, and he could see a green tree and a section of straw roof, as well as a small strip of blue sky with a white cloud like a feather.

Presently Luke heard somebody coming. He closed his eyes and lay quite still.

"It must be the girl," he thought.

"He looked at me," whispered the girl.

"So it *is* her," thought Luke.

"He was awake," the girl went on. "I'm quite certain."

"Poor boy," a woman answered in a low voice. "He's had a bad time, but now I begin to think God means him to live."

Luke lay still, thinking how nice it was to hear friendly words spoken about himself, Luke Janson from

Ullsthorp. It warmed his heart to hear them, and he opened his eyes to see who the speaker was.

"It must be the girl's mother," he thought.

The woman stood bending over him, with the girl out of sight behind her.

"Are you alive?" the woman asked at once. She must have had the words ready before he opened his eyes.

Luke found it strange to have to answer a question like that. In any case, he seemed unable to make his mouth answer, so he did the next best thing by looking up at her and trying to nod.

The woman turned to the girl. "Fetch some milk, Birgitta," she said.

"Ah yes, ah yes," she said with a sigh when the girl had gone. Then she squatted on her haunches at Luke's side and stroked his hair. "Now I do believe you're going to live," she said.

She sat for a little gazing thoughtfully in front of her. "You've been lying here so long that I was beginning to have my doubts," she explained. "We've seen so many people go to God," she added. "Poor boy! Ah yes! But now you must drink a little, and you'll be all right. Master Martin has put herbs on your foot to drive the pain away!"

The girl returned, carrying a black earthenware bowl. She came and held it at arm's length in front of her, as if she were afraid to come too close.

Luke drank. It was fresh milk and tasted good. Afterward he felt a little better. Perhaps there were herbs mixed in the milk—it seemed to taste so different from usual. He lay quite still and felt his body waking up and becoming stronger.

Soon the girl came back with another bowl. "Here you are!" she said.

It was a gray barley gruel. The girl helped him to a little of the gruel with a wooden spoon, while her mother supported his back.

The woman kept talking to him all the time, telling how she had had six children before the plague came and how she now had only Birgitta.

Luke was unable to answer. "She's talking as much to herself as to me," he thought.

Meanwhile, it was good to eat some food again. He just nodded once or twice to the woman to show that he was listening. But, in fact, he was listening with only one ear because now he had begun thinking about something else, something important. The thoughts started up in his head of their own accord as soon as he was fully awake.

He wanted to know how long he had been here. "How long?" That was as much as he could say at one go, but it was enough.

"Seven days," answered the woman. "It was lucky for you that Master Martin was out in the town that day and that you fell right at his feet—or you would have been trampled to pieces or dragged out of the town—people have become so frightened since the plague . . ."

"Where's Hanna?" asked Luke suddenly. The whole thing was beginning to come back.

"Hanna?" repeated the woman. "Is that your sister?"

"Yes," said Luke, nodding, but then he began to have doubts. "No," he corrected himself. "Almost," he explained. "We were together, you see, and we were trying—she was trying—we were both trying to catch Crutch-Olaf because the floggers had taken her."

"The floggers?"

"Yes, the people with whips . . . and drums . . . and flutes. They looked dreadful with all that blood on their backs."

"Wait a minute!" exclaimed the woman. "So you've lost a girl?"

He nodded.

"And she's called Hanna?"

"Yes."

"And she's 'almost' your sister?"

Another nod.

"How can she be 'almost' a sister?" The woman looked thoughtful.

Luke did not answer—things like that are beyond explanation. Either you understand or you don't, however often it's explained.

"And she was with you the day you came here?"

"I don't know. Yes, I think she let go . . ."

"Well, I know nothing about her," said the woman. "But maybe Master Martin knows something."

Shortly afterward the woman left, and Luke was alone with Birgitta. "Is that your mother?" he asked.

"Yes."

"She's nice," he said. "But where's Master Martin?"

Luke wondered if Master Martin was a priest since they put "Master" in front of his name.

"Father's in the church."

"Is this the priest's house, then, that I've come to?"

The girl laughed. "Yes, don't you like it? Isn't it good enough for you here?"

"Yes, I don't mean that." Luke was a little bit sheepish because she was laughing at him. "It's only that I'm not used to being in a priest's house," he added. "It's quite new for me."

"Where are you used to being, then?"

Luke could hear the curiosity in the girl's voice. She came right up to him and squatted beside him.

"I'm used to being out!" he answered.

"How do you mean 'out'?"

"Out on the roads or in the woods!"

The girl gasped, "Aren't you ever at home?"

"No, I just live out under the sky and the clouds and the trees. Because I'm on a long journey—a very long journey."

"Right to the end of the world?"

"Yes, almost."

"But don't you live anywhere?"

He shook his head. "I used to live at home with Father and Mother. Then . . ." Luke stopped speaking and sighed.

The girl nodded gravely. "Ah yes, the plague," she said. "We've had the plague here, too. That was why Mother said you were to stay here."

"How do you mean?"

"Why, because she said you were just the same age as our Francis was. And Mother misses Francis terribly—and Ben and Lena and Nis and little Kirsten. That's why she said you were to stay here and sleep in Francis's place."

The girl looked closely at Luke. "Are you a tease?" she asked. "Francis was a tease—and Nis—they were the worst. I miss Kirsten most."

Luke shook his head. He was not certain if he remembered it or if it was something he had dreamed: a priest in black, who had said they were to come and carry him in. It was so long ago that he could not remember it clearly.

He lay still for a long time, looking at the girl. Then suddenly he asked, "Do you know where Hanna is?"

Birgitta pursed her lips and shook her head.

"I want to go and find her," said Luke. "I'm going out as soon as I can get up. She can't simply have vanished."

But it was many days before he could go and look for Hanna.

If he hadn't been thinking of Hanna all the time, he would have enjoyed his stay in the priest's house. Master Martin was a kind man, and Birgitta's mother was so good to him that at times it was almost as if he were at home again.

Luke knew that priests weren't allowed to marry, so Birgitta's mother could not be the lady of the house. Yet even if Birgitta's mother was only the priest's housekeeper, she was never spoken of except as "Master Martin's Mary"—although certain people sometimes added something he did not quite understand, beyond the fact that it was unkind. All the same, the priest's house was just like any other house.

Luke spoke of Hanna so often that Master Martin made inquiries about her in the town, but he learned nothing. The terrible flagellants had gone on their way, and nobody knew where.

Had Hanna managed to recover Crutch-Olaf before

they left? Or had she gone after them? Had they captured her and taken her with them when she tried to recover the horse? There was nobody who could answer Luke's questions.

Once he heard Master Martin and his housekeeper talking about him. It was about the time Luke began hobbling around in the house. He was feeling a little faint and sat down on a chair in a room at one end of the house. The shutter stood ajar, and he heard them just outside, in the apple orchard.

Birgitta's mother seemed sad. She often cried, and Luke realized it was because of the plague and her dead children. In those days tears were frequent with everybody.

"We still have Birgitta," he heard Master Martin say. "And of course the boy is still here. Where else can he go, poor lad?"

"Ah, if only he would stay." She sighed. "It's almost like when we had Francis." There was silence for a while, and Luke knew that it was because she was weeping.

"No, it wouldn't be right," she went on. "But then it wouldn't be so empty here. If only he would stay, then Birgitta, too, would have somebody to cling to."

"In that case, we must begin by finding the girl he keeps talking about—Hanna! He thinks of nothing else, day or night. You can see he'd be quite different if she came."

"We could easily have them both," she said. "And if it's God's will, we shall find her."

"Yes," said the priest, "it's true we could easily have them both." It sounded as if he were thinking of something else.

"Isn't there anything you can do to find her?" Birgitta's mother spoke with great emphasis.

"Yes," the priest answered. "But I'm wondering if I shan't get an answer soon from Master Jasper at Ansthorp. I asked him about the girl in my last letter. And I told him I'd heard that the flagellants had gone his way."

"Perhaps they've passed through Ansthorp. In that case, Master Jasper will have seen them. And he would certainly have noticed if there was a child with them."

Luke sat as quiet as a mouse and held his breath. Was it possible? Would they soon hear about Hanna? His spirits rose, and he waited eagerly for the answer.

Master Martin had said nothing yet about a letter, not to Luke at least, but a few days later Luke himself went out in the town to ask about Hanna. It was the first time he had been out since his illness.

It was his intention to search for Hanna everywhere, all over the town. Indeed, he had even told Birgitta that he would search through the whole world until he found her because when he found Hanna, everything would be good again.

In the town he asked people if they had seen the flagellants and if they had had a little brown horse with them and a girl of his own age in a brown dress, with long dark hair done in a braid. But people are strange in towns. Some would not even stop to hear his questions; others advised him to leave madmen like that to their own devices. Nobody knew of a girl who had been anywhere near the flagellants.

He was tired when he returned to the priest's house

that day, but he was determined to go on looking another day, since now he was too tired to be able to do any more.

That afternoon Luke was sitting, lost in thought, under an apple tree in Master Martin's orchard. As he sat there, he noticed how busily Master Martin's bees were flying in and out of their hives. There was a continuous buzzing among the trees. As long as you sat quite still, the bees would fly past without stinging you. They were in constant movement over their work. Each bee fetched a little honey, so little as to be almost invisible. Luke remembered his father saying that bees can fill a hive just by keeping at it all the time, without stopping. The amount each bee brings is little more than nothing and hardly seems to make any difference, but all the same it grows and grows.

"Learn from the bees! You must never give up—even if you think you are getting nowhere!" That was what his father had said to him long ago. It was incredible to Luke how everything had changed since last summer. It seemed so long ago that the whole world must have grown old in the meantime. "Keep going!" his father used to say, and doubtless his father's father had said the same to his father, and his father's grandfather to his father's father, and so on, right back to the beginning of the world.

Luke sighed. It was all very well to keep going, but how? All he knew was that he had to find Hanna. How, he did not know. He had asked and asked, but all in vain. How was he to hold out?

Without knowing it, Luke had folded his hands. He

sat under the apple tree in the priest's orchard and prayed aloud for help to find Hanna.

Master Martin, too, was in the orchard, standing a short distance away.

"Luke," said the priest.

Luke raised his head and hurriedly rubbed his eyes.

"I understand," said the priest. "It doesn't matter. You can cry if you want to."

Luke was a tiny bit afraid of the priest. He did not answer.

Master Martin lifted his black robe a little and sat down heavily on the grass, with his back against the rough trunk of an apple tree. He was a stout man and breathed heavily when he sat down.

Luke wondered what he was going to say.

"You're thinking about her, the girl Hanna," the priest began. His once black beard was turning gray, and his hair lay like a white wreath around the close-shaven top of his head.

"I've had a letter from Master Jasper in Ansthorp," he continued slowly, as if he had to draw up each word from the depths of his being. Then he told how the flagellants had passed through the village of Ansthorp and how the people there had driven them out with stones—there was nowhere where they were left in peace. "Master Jasper thinks they must be on their way to the German lands."

Luke waited eagerly for the priest to continue. His heart was beating so violently that he could almost hear it. But Master Martin brooded for a long time on what he should say, and Luke grew impatient.

"Was . . . was Hanna with them?" he whispered.

"I wrote and asked Master Jasper if he had seen a girl in a brown dress with a long braid and whether they had a horse and cart with them."

Luke found himself looking into the priest's eyes. They were so mild and friendly that it did one good just to look at them. He had never noticed before what good, gentle eyes the priest had.

"I know, of course, how much you want to find Hanna again," the priest went on. "That was why I wrote and asked Master Jasper."

"But . . . but was she there—did he know anything, Master Jasper?"

The priest slowly shook his head. "No, he hadn't seen any girl, and he wrote that he had asked after her in Ansthorp, but nobody had seen any girl. However, the flagellants had two horses harnessed to a cart."

"Yes, but . . ." said Luke and then stopped, for what could he say? He knew only that Hanna was gone. Nobody knew where she was.

"Well, we can be thankful that she hasn't gone with those terrible people," said Master Martin, "because by now they must be right down in Holstein. She's more likely to be somewhere in this area. Perhaps she's still in this town, like yourself." Master Martin looked for a long time at Luke without saying anything.

"Of course he can't say it," Luke thought. Hanna couldn't be in this town because if she had been, Master Martin would have heard about it long ago; people would have been certain to tell him about a thing like that. And he can't say what's in his mind about all the lonely places out in the country. Since the plague a person could go for miles without meeting anyone. So many people were dead or fled, even if it was much less bad here than where Luke came from. It could be very difficult to find a girl who had left the town—nobody would know which way she had gone and whether she had been on her own. Besides, a girl as old as Hanna could easily have mingled with the flagellants, without Master Jasper or anyone else in Ansthorp noticing. For that matter, she could have been hidden in the cart.

"Yes, but what am I to do then?" asked Luke. "You see, I . . . I want to find her. You see, she's . . ." He stopped again. How could he say what he really meant? How could he explain who Hanna was and how much she meant to him? Even if he tried, he would never succeed. It wouldn't mean anything if he just said that he had found her all on her own in a village where everyone else was either dead or gone away. Nor could he explain that he had gone with her for a long time, on a very long journey, that they had been together at a time when it looked as if they were the only people in the world.

It wouldn't help to say things like that because they're not the kind of things that anyone else can understand. And he couldn't say that the whole world had become empty since Hanna had gone—a podgy fourteen-year-old girl who had never known her father or her mother. How could he explain that his world had grown sad and empty because she had been half of his world? And it would sound strange if he were to say that many times a day it was just as if he could hear her voice quite distinctly.

No, you couldn't say things like that to anyone, and how could he bring himself to say that he had cried almost as much when Hanna disappeared as he had done when all his family at home died of the plague?

The sound of Master Martin's voice made Luke jump, he was so far away in his own thoughts. "We will pray for Hanna, that we may find her again," said the priest. "Meanwhile, you must go on looking for her. And I will tell my congregation once again that they must tell me if they see her here in this town. If no one has seen her, you must go out into the countryside and search there. From here the road goes to Ansthorp, and then to Ribe. You can follow the road, and ask at every place you come to."

The priest paused and put his hand on Luke's shoulder. "But you are also welcome to stay here," he added kindly. "You can stay here as long as you want. Just go out looking for her and then come back again—all the way from Ribe if necessary. If you find Hanna, both of you can stay here."

Again Luke noticed Master Martin's eyes, and he knew that he need not be afraid of him—the priest was a man he could always rely on.

"Thank you," was all he said, although he would have liked to say much more.

"You know of course," the priest went on, "that God has taken many of my . . . of our children. It would gladden our hearts to have you, and Hanna too, in their place."

For a long time the only sound under the tree was the buzzing of the industrious bees.

At last Luke said, "But Uncle Nicholas at Ribe. We . . . I would like . . ."

Master Martin nodded. "Yes, I remember what you told me. And you must decide for yourself," he said quietly. "I just wanted you to know that there's room for you here—for both of you."

Although Master Martin asked over and over again in the church, there was no news of Hanna. No one knew anything about her. Luke was beginning to feel quite fit again, and he waited with growing impatience.

One day he took a little walk outside the town. A field of rye stretched out in front of him. As he walked, he picked a few ears and ground them in his hands so that the grain fell out in his palms. He tasted them: they were almost ripe! Then he knew that it was harvest time, and soon the summer would be over. He must leave for Ribe now!

He said to Master Martin, "I must go. If you will show me the way to Ansthorp, I will go there, then to Ribe, asking about Hanna all the way."

"Yes, I have expected this for a long time," said Master Martin. "And you must do what you think right. Mary will put some food together for you."

Early the next morning the priest accompanied Luke out of the town. They climbed together out of the valley in which the town lay. The hill commanded a wide view over the land to the west. Woods and fields spread over the hills and along the valley.

"Just follow the road, my boy," said the priest, "till you come to Ansthorp. There you can call on Master Jasper. He lives right beside the church. And if you continue west again, you will come to Ribe."

"How far is it to Ribe?"

"If you have a horse you can easily do it in a couple of days, but if you are on foot and have to keep asking your way, it can take you many days. Now you must go in peace, and may heaven help you. And remember that you can always come back to us in the priest's house."

Luke nodded silently as the priest gave him his hand in farewell.

"Go now," he said. "I want to see how you look as you walk through the land. Then I can think of you and pray for you."

Luke could not bear to say good-bye. He turned and set out west. Many times he turned and looked back to see Master Martin standing in the morning sun and waving. Finally the road turned downhill a little, so that he would soon be unable to see the priest any longer. When he turned and waved for the last time, he could see Master Martin with his arms raised, as if in blessing, and that was the last he saw of the priest.

He continued briskly on his way, thinking of Hanna and trying to work out what she would have done next. If she had really caught Crutch-Olaf, what would she have done? When she didn't find Luke, what would she have done? He would ask at every village between here and Ribe.

CHAPTER 11

Between the hills lay a little cluster of gray houses. It seemed as if they had huddled together here in the valley for shelter against the winds that roamed the land. They were ordinary mud-built houses, with slightly crooked doorframes and roofs that sat askew.

Outside one of the houses stood a man. He was standing beside a long stable wall, and beside him the dungheap was thick with enormous weeds. It had stood there untouched for so long that it had almost blended into the earth.

The man was absorbed in his work. He was one of those people who have eyes in only one direction, so he never noticed what was going on behind him and that he had guests—or at least a guest, a silent spectator of his hard work.

Indeed the man was hard at work—work of a kind one attempts only once in a lifetime. He was using a block of granite so big and heavy that he needed both hands to hold it securely, and was scraping it slowly backward and forward over the mud wall. He had nearly finished. Only a single broad black streak of tar still remained on the yellow-gray mud wall.

The peasant paused in his unusual task. It seemed as if many thoughts were whirling around in his limited brain, so many that he had reached a deadlock. The stone fell to the ground between the nettles and the enormous docks, but instead of picking it up again, the man stepped back a pace and examined the wall. The eaves were so low that he had to bend his head to see under them.

The wall showed a series of faint marks. It was still clear what they had been, but soon the last traces would vanish. The man straightened up and gave a deep sigh. Then he turned and glanced around at random.

Only then did his eye light on the freckled boy standing behind him. He rubbed his eyes and glared at the boy from under his bushy eyebrows. He spat and turned angrily back to the stable wall, picked up his stone, and resumed his scraping operations. Up and down went the stone over the last black snake of tar that reared up on its tail from the ground to the eaves.

It took him quite a long time, for the black marks were not easy to remove, but at last he finished. Once more he stepped back to see if everything was in order. Not a trace of the black marks must be allowed to remain!

He appeared satisfied with his work. At all events, he threw the stone down. It hit the ground with a thud and lay in its accustomed place. No one could tell when that stone would be needed again. It was a gray stone with a flat surface well suited to scraping off tar.

The peasant crossed himself, and the stone, and the

farm—invisible crosses that could never be erased. Then once again he inspected the wall over its entire length.

"You're not from here," he said without looking at the boy, but fully aware that he was still standing there.

"If I was, I wouldn't be standing here," Luke answered quietly. Surely that was obvious. And the man would not have been asking questions.

The peasant said no more. He had an inscrutable air, as if the muscles of his face had been fastened so tight that he could never smile again. The boy knew from experience that a taciturn peasant like that could go for a long time without opening his mouth. So for the sake of saying something he added, "I'd have gone home!"

The peasant turned around angrily and glared at the boy with his small, blinking eyes. Despite the man's surly manner, the boy could see a flicker of curiosity behind his sunburnt brow.

"Eh?" It sounded almost like a grunt.

"I'd have gone home," the boy repeated slowly and carefully. There was no point in making his impatience too apparent. And he added, "To eat and sleep, and maybe to tell something about where I've been."

"Mm!" The peasant turned and started to go. He wasn't exactly young or exactly old, but something in between; a gnarled man, who walked slowly, having exhausted whatever supply of speed he might once have had.

At the corner he stopped and spat. Then he glanced up at the clouds and over at the other houses in the village. Finally, before disappearing, he said, turning halfway toward the boy, what sounded like "Hum!"

The boy waited for a while, uncertain what to do.

Then he followed the peasant as far as an open door. No doubt the man had gone in there.

At this moment a woman came to the door. She looked in each direction, as if she knew that someone was coming. Then her eye fell on the boy. "Come in here, boy!" she said briskly.

"Thank you."

In the farm Luke was first given something to eat, then told he could stay there for the night. In return, he told a little about his adventures. Then he asked if they had seen a girl go past, a girl in a brown dress and with a pigtail.

No, there had been plenty of people on the roads since the plague let up, the woman told him, but very few children and no girls.

Luke slept there that night, and he slept like a log. The next morning he continued west until he reached the next village. Here he made exhaustive inquiries before going on his way.

And so the days passed as he went from village to village asking and asking until he felt satisfied with his day's work.

In this part of the country there were people in every village—not always many, but always some. Usually they were busy with the harvest, a poor, plague-year harvest. Mostly he was allowed to sleep in one farm or another. Only once did he have to stay in a deserted one because no one would take him in. Fear was still strong! That night he'd slept in an empty barn.

What worried him was that he got no news of Hanna. No one had seen a girl on her travels. On the other hand, he kept hearing about a boy who was out on the highways like himself. In fact, the country seemed full of boys on their way somewhere or other.

Eventually he came to the village of Ansthorp, where he quickly found the church. Built on to the churchyard wall was a house with lopsided wings, which must be the priest's house.

Master Jasper gave him a warm welcome, especially since he came with an introduction from Master Martin. Luke was given food and allowed to spend the night in the priest's house. Master Jasper told him a little about Ansthorp, which lay at a road junction, with one road going south toward the German lands and another going west toward Ribe.

When Master Jasper had to go to his church, Luke went with him. In the churchyard there were many mounds of earth. All the same, Master Jasper said, the plague had not been as bad here as it had been in the west, where, or so he had heard, many villages were completely abandoned.

"Yes," said Luke, "that's true!"

The priest began praying aloud, and Luke rejoiced to hear him asking for help to find Hanna. Next Master Jasper sat on his chair and read a big black book while Luke wandered around looking at the inside of the church. It was much like other churches he had seen, but behind the altar was a ladder leading up to the loft. Luke clambered slowly up it, partly from habit, partly for another reason.

Up under the roof it was almost pitch dark, and he felt his way cautiously across the loft. His legs simply carried him forward while his mind was elsewhere.

He pictured another church loft, a long way away. Ah, how happy he had been then because he had met Hanna! What was it she used to do? Ah, yes. Whenever something was beyond her, she used to pray. And now he, too, began to pray . . .

As he was about to climb down the ladder again, something fell to the ground. He must have kicked something lying just beside the trapdoor.

He descended, wondering once again what he should do next. Should he turn around and go back to Master Martin in case Hanna had turned up? Or should he continue as far as Ribe and see if she was there? Perhaps that would be the best.

Of course *she* didn't know where *he* was either. If she had been looking for him, she certainly hadn't found him! And what else could she do, assuming she wanted to see him again, except go to Ribe?

Suppose the flagellants had taken her with them? In that case, he could only hope that somehow she might escape their clutches, and then she would surely make for Ribe!

Suddenly it was quite clear to Luke that the only chance of finding Hanna was to assume she had gone to Ribe because she on her side would assume that he would sooner or later go there. In Ribe she would ask for his Uncle Nicholas.

Luke had stopped on the lowest rung of the ladder. If only she had given those terrible flagellants the slip, he thought, she must by now be on her way to Ribe. Indeed, she might even be there already!

As he stepped off the ladder, his bare toes touched

an object, and he groped with his foot over the paving stone. What was it? He bent down and picked something up. Oh, was that all? Luke turned it over in his hand and was about to throw the thing away again—it was only a little comb—when suddenly he seemed to hear someone say, "Oh dear, now I've broken a tooth."

He peered at his find with new interest. It was just a small, bent bone comb, and precisely one tooth was missing. "That needn't mean anything," he thought. "There must be millions of bone combs in the world—and there must be many with broken teeth."

Afterward, though, he showed the comb to Master Jasper. The priest didn't recognize it, and he was positive it couldn't have been lying on the church floor for very long or he would have seen it—he walked around the church every day.

"Does anyone ever go up in the loft?" Luke asked. He had suddenly remembered that an object fell as he was crawling through the trapdoor. "It must have fallen from up there," he added.

"Not very often," said the priest. "The thatcher has to go up from time to time, but he's the only one. As it happens, he's been up there quite recently, patching the roof. That's why the ladder's still there."

"How long has it been there?" Luke's heart was beating violently over a thought that had just occurred to him.

"Oh . . . three or four days, I'd say."

"Does the thatcher use a comb like that?"

Master Jasper laughed. "Piers Thatcher? No, he'd have no use for it—he's as bald as an egg!"

"Church lofts were her favorite place," Luke explained. "She felt safer there. And it's a funny thing this comb being like hers. If she's been here . . ."

". . . someone must have seen her." Master Jasper completed the sentence for him. "I'm going around the village to ask—it won't take long."

"I must hurry after her," Luke said, "if I'm to catch up with her. She's sure to be on her way to Ribe—looking for me, I expect."

"Go to the house first," Master Jasper advised, "and tell my housekeeper that you need some food to take with you. Meanwhile, I'll go and ask if anyone has seen her, your Hanna. Because if she's really been here, somebody is bound to have seen her!"

When the priest returned, all he could say was that no one had seen a girl passing through the village. Indeed, the only person who had noticed a stranger during the last three or four days was an old woman who was unable to sleep and who often went for a little walk in the early morning. She had done so two days ago and had seen a boy—or perhaps a young man—coming past her house. But whether he had come from the church she was unable to say.

"Never mind," said Luke. "It's not certain that anyone would have seen her, even if she had been here. What is certain is that unless somebody's holding her as a prisoner, she'll make for Ribe. And it would be like her to go up to the church for a sleep—she was always fond of churches. I must hurry. Perhaps I shall overtake her on the way to Ribe—I wouldn't like her to get there first."

That same evening Luke arrived at the next village—a tiny little village. The church was small, too—a modest little building with a thatched roof. He arrived just as the church bell was ringing the sun to bed.

"It's best to go straight to the point," thought Luke, making straight for the churchyard. It was overgrown with grass and weeds, and even the new plague graves were covered in greenery.

In one corner of the churchyard stood a bell tower. Huge black beams had been cut and nailed together in a series of enormous crosses. At the top, under a straggly straw roof, hung the bell, swinging heavily to and fro. The man operating the bell rope was short and thick-set. He stood there between the beams, pulling calmly on the rope so that at regular intervals the sound of the bell was wafted out over the countryside.

Luke was tired today. He had walked all day, and now he sat on the grass waiting for the bell ringer to finish. For a moment he thought how strange it was to be sitting with the dead in the ground beneath him. He was not afraid, however; one thing he had learned from his experiences was that there was nothing to fear from the dead.

How should he set about questioning the bell ringer? People were so reluctant to say anything, and he was in a hurry! It was as if something were tugging at his elbow.

Now the ringing was almost over; the final strokes came evenly at long, regular intervals: three strokes, then a pause, then three more strokes. There was nothing lame or halting about this bell, as there so often is. The bell ringer was a confident, strong man, neither crippled nor deaf!

"God's peace!" Luke called in greeting. He had gotten up and walked across to the bell ringer.

"Thanks!" growled the other.

"That's a fine bell you have here," Luke continued. "It has a lovely sound. It even seems to be saying something!"

"Yes," the bell ringer said, nodding, "it does that, but there are very few people left to hear it nowadays."

He peered at Luke. "Do you understand it, then?"

"Ye-es, it's telling people to come to church. 'Come in, come in,' it's saying!"

"You think so?"

"Oh yes. And then everyone wants to go into the church because the bell is calling to them."

"Not nowadays," answered the bell ringer with a sigh. "There are so few people here. But you're welcome to go in!"

Luke was glad; he felt he had to go into every church he came to. He followed the bell ringer into the church and stopped at the great oak door and gazed at the huge, solid lock.

"Do you lock the church at night?" he asked.

The bell ringer shook his head. "The house of God should always be open—like heaven!"

Luke wandered around the church looking at everything: the windows, the font, the altar, and the austere cross on the wall. He looked to see if there was a ladder up to the loft, but there was no sign of one.

"Is it possible to go up in the loft?" he asked warily.

The bell ringer shook his head. "No!"

Luke looked all around to see if there was anywhere you might lie down and sleep. One place where you might lie down was over by the altar. There was a kind of cushion for the priest to kneel on—or rather a kind of footstool. It would not be comfortable to lie on. But what about the thick bench over by the outer wall?

"Do people ever come in here—I mean, at night?" he asked, trying to make it sound like an everyday question.

"Yes, every now and then. There's been so many people on the roads of late—during the plague. But now it seems to be coming to an end."

Luke noticed that the bell ringer crossed himself at the word "plague," and hastened to do the same himself.

"There hasn't been anyone . . . quite recently?"

"No. It's a long time since I saw anyone. But of course there could easily have been someone without my noticing. I don't notice everything, you know—there are so many other things you can think about when you're ringing!"

"I can understand that," said Luke. "It's the same when you're on the road: you keep thinking of all sorts of things, and you don't see what's in front of your nose."

"But wait a minute," added the bell ringer. "I think it was this morning, or perhaps it was yesterday morning, that a boy came past while I was ringing. I'm not quite certain if it was the church he came from. I was looking at Torkil's cows," he explained. "The old brindled cow is just going to calve, you see, and I thought it was limping as if there were something wrong with it. So it may well be that the lad had been in the church—only I can't see any trace of him."

"How big was he? Bigger than me or smaller?" asked Luke.

The bell ringer shook his head.

"I couldn't say. I just saw a boy walking past, close to the wall. He was wearing knee-breeches, but he was gone so quickly that that was all I noticed. By the time I'd finished ringing he'd disappeared down the road."

"Which road?" Luke asked hurriedly.

"To the west!" said the bell ringer.

Then he stood for a while looking at Luke. "And who are you, may I ask?"

"Oh," said Luke slowly, "I'm just a boy with no home. I'm on my way to Ribe to look for my Uncle Nicholas. But I've lost Hanna, and I think she must be on the way to Ribe. I keep dreaming about it."

"Poor boy," mumbled the bell ringer. "Come home with me. We've got food in the house, and Dorothea can give you something to eat." Luke was only too willing as he was tired and hungry.

The bell ringer's house proved to be an old farmhouse and Dorothea to be a young woman. She gave Luke a friendly welcome and a good meal. He could see that she was expecting a child. As they ate, she and the bell ringer talked a little. They spoke of the harvest, the plague harvest, and how meager it was because so little sowing had been done. But then there were fewer people to feed. And the animals! It was hard work catching them. They had become almost as wild as the animals in the forest. As for the weather, even that seemed to have been struck by the plague—at all events, it was far too dry.

Luke heard all this and asked how bad the plague had been in this village.

"It was bad," the bell ringer began. The young woman gave him a quick glance. He was silent for a while, then he sighed and continued. "Twenty people died in this village—that's half of us—and four of them . . . were mine."

Dorothea put her hand on his but said nothing. The bell ringer sighed again. "My three children and their mother. All I had." He sat still, blinking rapidly, with his eyes fixed on the roof.

Luke said nothing and resolved once again never to ask questions about the plague.

Dorothea must have thought he had been silent too long because she said, "No, we're not married yet—Martin and me. It's not possible at present because our priest died, too, and we haven't got a new one yet."

Luke nodded and said nothing.

"Of course we could go and find another priest," she went on, "but it's not easy just now. We keep hoping and praying that a new priest will come. And he'd better come before . . ." Dorothea sighed and wiped her eyes with the back of one hand, the other still resting on Martin's arm. Her voice died away into a whisper.

"She'd have liked to say more," thought Luke.

"I found Dorothea out in the forest," said Martin the bell ringer, who was evidently a farmer also. "She had come from far away."

"But we *shall* get married," Dorothea interrupted, "as soon as we get a priest out here."

She smiled as she said this, and the man agreed. "Yes," he said, smiling at her. "Life's not so bad when there are two of you to endure it," he added, caressing her bare arm.

"Perhaps God will be really good to us," said Dorothea. She was looking at the man and seemed unconscious of Luke's presence. "Perhaps you'll even have three children again."

Luke sat there, as though far away. For a long time nobody spoke. Finally he asked, "How far is it to the next village west?"

"Oh, it's not all that far," said the man. "If you leave here tomorrow morning, you'll be there by midday. But you can stay here and sleep and be on your way in the morning."

"Thank you," said Luke, "I'd like to do that. My legs are worn out with all the walking I've done."

CHAPTER 12

Luke was awakened by someone calling his name! He sat up, listening in the dark. He could just make out the smokehole showing up as a light patch under the ridge of the roof, but now he could not hear anything. Earlier it had been quite clear that somebody had been calling to him. Or was it something he had dreamed?

A little confused, he rubbed his eyes. He could see nothing, and even if he held his breath and listened, he could still hear nothing except for the breathing of the people asleep in the room. He gave a sigh. Yes, it was evidently just a dream. It had seemed just as if . . .

Luke lay down again but was unable to sleep. He tried to recall the details of his dream. He could still hear the cry quite distinctly inside his head, and the voice was unmistakable. It drew him up out of his bed of hay in the warm house and out into the cool night. Before he knew what he was doing, he was on the road.

He had crept very quietly from the house, stolen on tiptoe past the church, and taken the road to the west. At first his conscience bothered him. He ought not to have left those two good people without saying good-bye and thanking them for his board and lodging, but it was as if he'd had no choice.

Once out in the gray night, he was soon wide awake. He sniffed at the scent from the trees and knew it would soon be morning. The night wind sighed gently in the leaves, as if lulling itself to sleep. In the sky to the east came a faint glimmer of light like the embers of a bonfire. Now there was only one thought in his head: Forward!

At first his progress was easy as the road led through the fields adjoining the village. From time to time a solitary tree bobbed up out of the dark like a great animal standing there and looking out over the sleeping world. At one point he disturbed a herd of pigs that was sheltering under the trees. Alarmed by Luke's footsteps, they started up with a great hullaballoo of grunting. He himself was a little bit frightened by the din until he realized it was made by living pigs and not by unhappy spirits returning to earth as ghosts.

Presently he entered the forest. Even though it was nearly day, it was a good deal darker in here, where the path twisted up hill and down, in and out between the great gnarled oak trees. It was difficult to see the path in the twilight, and at first he had to go rather slowly. Gradually, however, the world emerged from darkness until he was able to hurry along the winding path. Indeed, it was a well-worn trail that twisted its way between the trees. Once upon a time, no doubt, there had been cart tracks also, but it was a long time since anyone had driven this way.

At one point he had to wade across a little stream. It

was not very wide or particularly deep, so the crossing went easily. On the other side of the stream, the forest came to an end, and soon Luke was once again walking through cultivated fields.

First came a field of rye. It was evidently self-sown because it grew sparsely and unevenly. The field was full of great patches of thistles. Without thinking, he took a handful of ears and rubbed them between his palms until he had a little handful of grain that was firm and ripe and tasted almost like bread.

He came to the top of a hill from which he could see the next village, nestling snugly down in a hollow. On the other side of the hollow was a little hillock, on which the church stood. It looked just like a great gray hen keeping watch over her chickens—the houses down in the hollow.

It was still early in the morning. The sun was not yet up, and the people were not yet up either. He passed through the village without seeing a soul, although in one place he aroused a dog, which went on barking at him for a long time.

At last he was there at the church. It was, of course, the church he was aiming for, yet if anybody had asked him why he wanted to visit it, he would have been unable to answer. He just did.

He knew he had to go to the church here—and every church he came to. Perhaps it was that dream, or perhaps it was something else, something somewhere inside him.

When he reached the churchyard wall, he stopped and wiped the sweat off his forehead. It had been a long and tiring walk!

He began counting on his fingers to see how many churches he had been in since the day he waved good-bye to Master Martin. "Let's see—this must be the seventh!" He would go in shortly after he had rested for a moment.

The stones of the churchyard wall were still damp with dew and cold to the touch. He shivered when he sat on them. He only intended to sit for a moment, to prepare himself. When he had been in the church, he would go down to the village and ask the usual questions. For a moment he sat with closed eyes. ". . . help me to find Hanna . . . I'm so lonely, so lonely."

He gazed around the churchyard at the graves and the church itself. It was made of massive stones with small windows high up. The roof was of straw. In short, it was almost exactly like the church at home in Ullsthorp, but then people built churches the same way all over the country. The door was black, and the bell hung from a black beam projecting from the gable right up under the roof.

He gave a sudden start when he saw a person standing by the door. He hadn't noticed the door opening, so he was uncertain where the stranger had come from. It was a boy of about his own age, with brown hair and wearing knee breeches. He was standing with his back to Luke, gazing out over the village.

"Ah," thought Luke, "it must be the boy I keep hearing about so often. Perhaps he has some inkling where Hanna is!"

Luke had, in fact, thought a good deal about that boy. He was evidently traveling in the same direction, and perhaps they would be company for each other—assuming he was someone Luke could talk to.

"I must go and ask him," thought Luke.

He must have made an awkward movement in getting up. A small stone fell from the wall.

The strange boy turned around quickly and looked straight at him. For a long time he stood quite still, just looking.

Luke was looking, too. There was something odd, he thought, something wrong somewhere. Then the strange boy began walking.

"He's coming over here," thought Luke.

At first the boy walked slowly and hesitantly, then faster and faster until finally he broke into a run.

Luke slid down from the wall and took a few steps toward the other. He felt quite dizzy. For a moment he wondered if the whole thing was a dream—in which case he would soon wake up. Was it? Or wasn't it?

"Luke!" the other shouted. "Luke, so it's really you! You're here—you've come . . . !"

"No," thought Luke, "it's no dream." And that was the last thought he had time for.

"Hanna . . . why . . ."

It was a long time before either of them could say another word. Luke could not remember ever having had such a hug in his life. He was laughing and crying over it at the same time. Hanna was doing the same. It was the first time for many a day that she had been able to cry and laugh with someone who cared about her—and that was worth laughing and crying over.

She forgot the many days and nights she had spent on her own, and Luke forgot how tired he was after walking and running so much last night instead of sleeping. At all events, he forgot it as they went hand in hand through the churchyard and out over the village fields. He did not even remember how tired he was when they reached the next stretch of forest.

They continued on their way, straight through the forest and out the other side where the landscape was different. The hills and woods came to an end, and the flat land stretched for miles. They walked on and on, saying little, happy just to be walking hand in hand.

In time, they came to a river. The road led right down to the water's edge, but the water looked deep. There was certainly no ford at this point. Just off the road was a group of low bushes, where they sat down for a rest.

Luke was happy at having found Hanna again, but by now the first excitement had died down. So instead of saying how happy he was, he asked, "Why are you dressed as a boy?"

"People are so brazen. That's why," was all she would say.

"What happened to you that time?"

Hanna sat down and took something out of her bag. She, too, was happy, so happy that she could not imagine why Luke wanted to ask questions since now everything was all she could wish. What was it Grandma Miller had said? Hanna sat there smiling. Her thoughts were far away, and she never heard Luke's question.

"What happened to you," he repeated, "the time they were flogging themselves?"

She looked happily at him. Then, with a great effort, she forced herself to remember. "Ah, yes, it was about Crutch-Olaf," she said. "I was trying to catch her, and

. . . and . . . then you disappeared. And there were so many people I couldn't find you anywhere when I looked for you."

"Yes, but did you catch the horse?" Without further ceremony Luke had started eating Hanna's dry bread, quite unaware of what he was doing.

"Yes . . . no, I mean. Or rather, I managed to catch hold of her reins and began leading her away, but . . . but . . ." Her voice faded away. She took out a broken knife and began cutting a piece of cheese.

"And then?" Luke was curious to know. Never mind if she didn't tell the whole story at one go—it would be something to talk about for a long time. Besides, he hadn't yet told her about his own adventures and where he had been for so many days.

"Well," said Hanna, "then they caught me—it was the man driving the horse. He said I was perfectly welcome to keep the old nag company, but he wanted to be there, too—and they'd certainly need to use the cart. Apart from that, I was welcome!"

Hanna's gaze rested steadily on Luke as he ate. She, too, had some food. She could hardly understand what had happened.

"I simply said I wanted Crutch-Olaf, my horse. Oh, and I said I didn't want him or the cart in the bargain. Just the horse, *my* horse!" She sighed and continued. "Then he turned nasty—and rude—and told me to keep my hands off his horse! He'd caught hold of one of my arms, or I'd have given him the slip."

"Why didn't you scream?" Luke asked dryly. "That's what girls always do to get their own way, and . . ."

"I did—and how! But I couldn't make myself heard

above the screaming and howling of all the others as they whipped themselves. You bet I screamed—for all I was worth," she said with a laugh. "Still, I managed to bite his finger and draw blood. And I kicked him wherever I could, on the legs and in the stomach, and then I punched his nose, and that was that, because then he really started using all his force!"

Luke looked at her with admiring eyes.

"I'm used to fighting, you see," Hanna added modestly, "from being with Claus Miller's boys—there were times when we went at it tooth and nail.

"Then he bundled me into the cart with their clothes and bread and hams and sausages and tied me up with my hands behind my back. 'Now you can stay with the old nag,' he said, 'you thief!' Yes, he actually called me a thief. 'Coming here stealing my horse. I'll teach you.' And he went on and on like that."

"So what did you do then?" asked Luke.

"Well, there wasn't really much I could do. At first I screamed and shouted that it was *he* who was the thief. But I couldn't make anyone hear because of all the others shouting and screaming. And then the townspeople started throwing stones at us. Look!" She pushed back her hair so that he could see her neck. "That was where a stone hit me."

Hanna could see that Luke was sleepy. He had stretched himself out on the grass under the bushes, a piece of bread still in his hand. It began to dawn on her how early he had arrived that morning.

"What time did you start walking this morning?" she asked.

"It was dark," Luke muttered.

"Have you been walking during the night?" she asked. "To . . . to find me?"

"Mm!"

Hanna took off her coat and laid it over him. "Sleep if you want to," she whispered. "There's plenty of time for talking—we won't ever be parted again."

"I wonder how far he's walked," Hanna reflected. "Well, he can have a good sleep now; he will be shaded from the sun for a long time."

A little way off a large black object was lying in the water. At first Hanna could not make out what it was, but on coming closer, she could see that it was a kind of big black sheet made out of thick, tarred pieces of wood. It had a familiar smell, a smell she associated with people. But what the object was she had no idea. It lay resting on the water like a great aquatic bird, with one side facing the bank. Hanna gave it a thorough inspection. From the dried horse droppings and cow pats, it was evident that there had been animals on it.

For a long time she sat on the grass beside the river, wondering what you did with a contraption like that. Finally her curiosity overcame her, and she gingerly put one foot on the mysterious thing. When nothing happened, she did the same with the other foot. The object supported her! She could feel it rocking gently on the water. And now she could see every inch of its surface. In one corner an iron chain was secured to a short, thick stake standing in the water close to the bank.

She liked the feeling of being rocked and cradled gently up and down. She took a few steps, enjoying the new sensation.

But what was a contraption like this used for? Could it be for . . . for—what was the word?—sailing? Hanna had heard about sailing and that one could sail on a contraption like this—indeed, that was precisely what she was doing at this moment. She was a little disappointed that there was no more to it. Ah, but of course it was standing still—things would be better when it moved!

She lay on her stomach and peered down into the water from a few inches' distance. How strange and full of life it was down there! Little black creatures were swimming around; some had many legs, others had none. And beneath them there was thick green grass, undulating in the flowing water.

Late in the afternoon the sun found its way in under the bushes, and its rays fell on Luke's face. Once or twice he curled up and turned the other way, but then he woke up.

At this moment Hanna returned from her walk along the river. At once she began telling him about the black thing for sailing on, and as soon as Luke was fully awake, they went down to the river to examine it more closely.

"Yes," Luke decided, "that's for sailing on all right. It's the kind of thing people use to get animals across the river if the water's too deep for them or if they're frightened. Perhaps *we* could sail on it?"

Hanna was eager to do so. "Just across to the other side?"

Luke, too, was longing to try, so they stepped aboard the raft. It gave a little under their weight, but they felt this only as a pleasant rocking.

Luke lost no time in exploring the raft. There were

some poles and planks lying on it, but these he ignored. Finally he came to the chain, which he lifted off the stake to free the raft. Still it didn't sail!

"How can we get it to sail?" asked Hanna. She was lying on her stomach, her arms plunged in the water up to the shoulders.

"By moving away from the land," Luke answered as he sat down on the side of the raft facing the bank. Then he placed his feet against the thick stake to which the chain had been fastened.

While he sat there pushing and causing the raft to rock agreeably, Hanna tried to find how deep the water was, using the poles for this purpose. The first two slipped from her grasp before she had touched the bottom with them. When they rose to the surface and began floating downstream, she was so amused that she did the same with the remaining poles.

"Look!" she exclaimed delightedly. "That's how one sails!"

Luke got up and helped her heave the last poles and planks into the water, till they were sailing down the river in a long row. And now Luke again put one foot against the stake. "Look!" he said. He was pushing the raft away from the land, and the gap between them grew bigger and bigger.

Now the land started to glide past the raft. Hanna laughed. "We've done it!" she shouted. "We're sailing!"

The raft swung around and came further out into the river. By now it was gathering speed steadily, and the children sat with bated breath. This was really something new, to sail!

"My bag!" Hanna shouted suddenly, when the first

excitement had worn off. "It's still there, where you were sleeping."

"We can't go and get it now." Luke scratched his neck. "Not just like that."

The raft was sailing away at full speed! It kept nicely out in the middle of the stream, with first one side in front and then the other. "It's lucky I've got my bag with me," said Luke, "so we shan't starve to death just yet."

"But . . . but how are we going to get back to the land again?"

Luke didn't answer. Instead he went up to the front end of the raft. It was a strange sensation. He felt a little giddy from the rocking of the raft and the way the land wandered past on both sides. Or rather bushes, reeds, and trees went past, while the fields turned slowly around and around. "I suppose we shall just have to wait till it comes in to the bank again."

"Yes, but how do they manage to sail this thing—the people who are used to it? Surely they can't just let it go on sailing until it chooses to go in to the land on the other side. They might go for miles without ever touching the land. Don't you think they must be able to steer it?"

"Yes, I suppose they must," said Luke. He was a little cross with himself for not having thought things out better and for not knowing how to steer the raft. "If only we knew how it works," he added. "Only we don't!"

"If we had . . . something," said Hanna slowly, "then we could steer it. A . . . a . . ." She broke off and stared at Luke. ". . . a pole!" she shouted.

Hanna threw herself flat and began beating her clenched fists against the planks. "Oh, I've been so stupid —stupid—stupid!" she shouted again and again.

Luke looked at her in surprise; he couldn't imagine what she was shouting about.

"What's the matter?" he asked cautiously, during a brief pause.

"Ugh," Hanna growled. Then she got up and gazed out into the water ahead of them. "There," she shouted, "there they are." She pointed.

"What are you talking about?"

"The poles! I threw them all in the water. We could have used them for steering to the shore by plunging them into the water—right down to the bottom."

"You're not so stupid after all," Luke muttered. "I'd never have thought of that."

"Only I was wise too late!" Hanna sighed. "That's often the way—you're wise after the event."

For a long time they sailed on in silence. The poles drifted farther and farther ahead.

Finally Luke said, "Well, at least we're better off than we were."

"How?"

"Why, because it's better to be sailing together on a raft than for you to be lying tied up in a cart in one place and me lying sick in another place!"

"That's true. But where do you suppose we're going?"

Luke didn't answer at once. He was looking back. He could still see the clump of bushes he had slept under. Or rather he thought it was the same clump, but it was too far away to be certain. As he gazed, the river made a bend and the bushes disappeared. Then he turned around and pointed ahead, saying, "Look!"

Hanna followed his gaze. All she could see was the

river and the sun, which was now quite low in the sky. "It will soon be night," she said.

But Luke wasn't thinking of that. "We're sailing west," he said.

"Well?" Hanna looked at him inquiringly. "West?"

"Ribe lies west from here!"

"Ah, I see. That means we're on our way! Even just lying here on this thing means the river's taking us on our way!"

"Exactly!" Luke grinned. "Maybe we could sail all the way to Ribe. And that's better than an old horse!" he added.

Hanna made no reply. She thought of Crutch-Olaf. She sat there and let her thoughts wander.

"It's deep here!" she said.

They lay face downward peering down into the water. In some places they could see the bottom far below; in others it was hidden by green stuff waving to and fro.

"Where do you suppose a river like this comes from?" asked Hanna.

"From a stream," Luke answered. He was repeating what he had once heard at home. "While it's small, it's a stream. Then it gets bigger and bigger until it becomes a great wide river like this. And finally, when it's finished being a river, it runs right out . . ." He stopped abruptly and looked at Hanna.

She was about to ask what was the matter when he continued. "We'd better find out how to land before . . ."

"Before?" Hanna was puzzled.

"Before the river runs right out into the sea!"

There was a long silence. Only the *glug-glug* of the water against the sides of the raft could be heard. The sun had set, and the air was turning cold.

"The sea," whispered Hanna. She was shivering already.

Luke nodded grimly. "All rivers run out into the sea!"

CHAPTER 13

Hanna and Luke had started sailing before the evening came, and they were still sailing when the sun set behind the thicket that was the only feature of the flat landscape.

Now it was beginning to grow dark. The stars accompanying the harvest moon shone bright and cold high over their heads. From time to time a star flashed across the sky, drawing a trail of light behind. They began to shiver, not only because it was growing cold, but also because they kept thinking of the mighty sea lying in wait for them somewhere, with its water that stretched to the ends of the world.

It was a strange night, sailing away on a raft they were unable to steer through a world that was quite foreign to them—the wet world of water. It was black all around the raft, and a steady gurgling rose from the cold water beneath them. The river seemed like a great black animal, carrying them onward through the night on its powerful back. The land slipping past was an endless dark shadow, as unseen and unfriendly as the Black Death.

To begin with, Hanna and Luke sat side by side talking, always about other things than their journey through the darkness with the shadows all around them. Hanna told Luke a little about how she had escaped from the flagellants. They had spent several days in a camp near the town; then one night she left them. They had all been so preoccupied with singing and dancing around their campfire that nobody noticed her slipping away.

They had forgotten to tie her hands, or they had left her alone on purpose, hoping she would vanish. Perhaps they had changed their mind about wanting to keep her—she had given them nothing but trouble. And perhaps the man who was supposed to be guarding her, and who had found her money, had been so busy counting it that he had forgotten to tie her hands. At all events, she had gone, wandering around in circles for a long time before she had found the right way to Ribe.

Luke told his adventures in turn. He talked about his stay with Master Martin, about Birgitta, about his bad foot, about Master Jasper, and the rest.

Then Hanna told more about her journey. She had become afraid of people and had done her utmost to avoid meeting them. She preferred going into churches.

Luke suddenly remembered the comb he had found and told Hanna about it. She reached for it in the dark and was certain it was hers.

"There's a little notch in one side," she said. "It must be mine. I lost it in the church loft at some village or other—it was so dark I couldn't find it again. I nearly always slept in churches," she explained. "I used to go there in the evening before it was dark and hurry away again before daylight. Nearly always before sunrise. I often slept some time during the day, too, under trees or bushes.

In one village an old woman told me that Ribe lay west. After that I always went in that direction."

"Were you frightened?" asked Luke.

"Yes." She sighed. "I was often frightened, especially at night."

"Was that why you wore boys' clothes?"

"Yes, the old woman gave them to me. She said things were easier for a boy nowadays and that I'd be wise to stop going into people's houses.

"After that it was the dark I was most afraid of," Hanna said after a pause. "But of course I knew I'd meet you somewhere—either in Ribe or on the way."

Luke was amazed. "How could you know that?" he asked. He remembered having been far from certain that he would ever find Hanna again.

Hanna laughed in the dark.

"I don't know! Perhaps because I'm a Sunday's child. But I knew all along that I'd find you."

At that moment it was as if a great hand gave them a violent push that sent them rolling around the raft! Luke found himself lying on his back, and when he looked up at the sky, the stars were going round and round.

Hanna reached out in the dark and grabbed his arm. "What was that?" she whispered, terrified. She squeezed Luke's arm painfully hard.

"I think we must have bumped into something."

Luke, too, spoke in a whisper. "A big stone perhaps." He held Hanna's hand in the darkness.

For a long time they sat in total silence, but nothing further happened.

"What if we fall in the water?" Hanna was breathless at the thought.

Luke had recovered from the worst of his terror. "We'd get wet," he said dryly. "And perhaps we'd stay there . . ." Deep inside, he was shuddering at the thought of the black, gliding water so close to them. What, indeed, if they fell in?

"We mustn't fall asleep," Hanna whispered. "If we did, we could roll off in our sleep. We must hold on tight to each other."

They tried various ways and at last found a good position sitting in the middle of the raft, back to back, with knees raised. This position gave them warmth as well as support. And to do things properly, they locked arms in a firm grip. Thus, they sat for a long time, while the raft glided through the night. But sitting like that for a whole night wasn't comfortable, and they began to ache in many places.

Hanna kept changing her position and occasionally rocking to and fro. When she did that, Luke rocked, too. He gave a little growl each time this happened.

"I'm aching," said Hanna. "I can't sit like this any longer."

"Turn around then," Luke muttered. He was almost asleep. "Or lie down!"

"You try," said Hanna. "It's easier said than done. If I lie down, you'll fall over, and if you lie down, I'll fall over."

"Fall over then," he said sleepily. "It doesn't matter!"

For a long time they kept shifting around on the hard planks.

"You mustn't let go," said Hanna.

"No," murmured Luke, but she was not certain that he had heard what she said.

"We can't afford to fall overboard," she thought. "I'd better do something about it."

Finally she found the solution. She tied one end of her belt around Luke's waist and the other around her own. "There!" she said. Then they lay quite still again.

"Luke!" she whispered.

"Mm?"

"Do you know what I think? I think we're going to make it to Ribe!"

But Luke didn't hear; he had fallen asleep.

"Let him sleep then," thought Hanna, and was soon asleep herself.

"Stop it!" Luke growled. Something or other kept hitting his head.

Hanna awakened and sat up with a start. She shivered and began turning her head, first one way, then the other. After that she cautiously touched her neck, as if to make sure she was still in one piece.

"Stop it yourself!" she said.

It was light now, and Hanna could see that Luke was doing nothing because he was lying peacefully asleep with his head resting in the dried horse droppings she had noticed yesterday.

"It may be the softest place there is," she thought, "but it's not very nice all the same."

A loud splash from the water at her side made her look up in surprise. Only then did she realize that the raft was no longer moving forward, but was lying at rest. It had drifted against a long row of stakes that stretched from one side of the river to the other, so close together that the raft could not get through. Above the stakes planks had been fastened, on which a person could walk. And indeed, someone was walking, or rather standing, on them at that moment.

It was a boy, a bare-legged boy, who peered at her, through the long fair hair that fell over his eyes, in the intervals between throwing pebbles, clods of earth, and sticks into the water or onto the raft.

As soon as he noticed her staring at him, he chanted:

"Slumber, slumber, golden curls;
Sleep is good for little girls.
Slumber, slumber, deaf to noise;
Sleep is good for little boys."

After which he made faces at her.

"Shut your trap!" The words burst from Hanna before she was sufficiently awake to contain her anger. That was just what Claus Miller's boys used to do if they wanted to tease her: sing or chant at her.

The boy merely grinned and dropped a specially big stone in the water, splashing both Hanna and Luke liberally.

"Why are you sailing so stupidly?" he shouted. "Just you wait! My dad will be out in a moment, and when he sees you here . . ."

"What's the matter?" Luke had awakened and sat up.

"The matter? Have you dropped out of the sky during the night by any chance? What a pair of yokels—with horse dung in your ears! You come sailing right into the millpond, and then you ask what's the matter!"

"Listen to me," Luke retorted. "I don't know what sort of brat you are. And I don't know where we are—we've been in so many places. But one thing I do know, and that is . . ." He drew an extra deep breath.

"Go on." The boy was straining to hear.

". . . and that is, that unless you behave properly, I'm going to come up there and beat the living daylights out of you!"

"Beat, did you say?" And he began chanting again.

> "Keep your hair on, little flea,
> It wouldn't be much use to me."

Luke grabbed hold of one of the planks and leaped up on the platform. It was not very wide, and there was no handrail. The next moment he seized the other boy around the waist as they balanced on the very edge. Luke panted, "Either you learn to treat strangers politely or I'll throw you in!"

The boy laughed. "Go on, then. I'll swim straight to the shore. Can you? Because if I go in, you go in with me!"

Hanna intervened. "Oh, stop it!" She knew Luke couldn't swim. "Can't you behave like normal, sensible human beings?"

"Hear, hear!" said the boy. "What do you mean by arriving at a strange place and starting to attack people?"

The two boys stood swaying on the narrow platform. Both were breathing heavily; both were red in the face.

"I've got your lead, little dog," the boy spat out. He tugged at the belt that was still tied to Luke's waist.

"I can't have tied it properly," thought Hanna.

"I could easily pull you into the water," he went on. "You're a fine visitor, attacking peaceful folk!"

Luke relaxed his grip a little, but kept one hand on the other's belt as a precaution.

"But I don't do that," he muttered. "By the way, my name's Luke, and this is Hanna."

"Hanna? Why is she dressed like a boy? Are you sweethearts or something?" the boy asked in one breath.

"We're on our way to a town called Ribe, to find my Uncle Nicholas," Luke continued, unruffled.

"Ribe!" interrupted the other. He stared at Luke through the slits of his eyes, trying to size him up. "You're *in* Ribe," he said. "Look!"

Neither of them had noticed the high stockade behind the trees lining the riverbank. Now they saw it with houses ranged behind it.

"Ribe?" Luke said slowly. "Is . . . is this Ribe?"

"Yes!" answered the boy. "And you're right by the mill—the north mill. If you listen, you can hear the mill whirring and clattering in there." He pointed ahead along the river. "And now you both know what it was you could hear all this time."

Hanna pricked up her ears. "Yes," she said eagerly,

"it's a mill. I can hear the millstone." To her it had a homey sound. "I want to get off this thing!"

"Of course!" Luke went down on his knees and stretched a hand down to her. A quick heave, and she was up on the platform with them.

She lost no time in getting off the platform onto the grass growing beside the river, and at once she decided never to sail again. It was a pleasure to be able to put both feet on firm ground.

"What will your old raft be used for now?" asked the boy. "You're not going to sail back on it, are you?"

Luke shrugged his shoulders. "I don't know."

"Can I have it?"

Luke saw his eagerness, and it occurred to him that now he had the advantage. How could he exploit it? His mind worked rapidly. "Yes," he said, "you can have it—if you'll help us find Uncle Nicholas!"

"Is that all?"

Then he stared again at Luke with his roguish, inquisitive eyes. "Did you say uncle?"

Luke nodded.

"Nicholas?"

"Yes!"

"Nothing else? Such as Nicholas Shoemaker or Nicholas Miller?

"No." That was as much as Luke knew.

"All the same, it's interesting," muttered the other.

"What do you mean?" asked Luke.

"Well, you see, there are . . ." and he began counting on his fingers, "there are—let me see—there are five, yes, exactly five Nicholases here in Ribe—or there were before the plague."

"There's nothing strange in that, is there?"

"No . . . no," the boy answered. "What *is* strange is that one of them is my father!"

"Your father?" Hanna and Luke held their breaths.

"That's right. Nicholas Miller of Ribe North Mill is my father."

Luke reflected on this. "If it's him," he said, with a wondering look at the other, "we must be cousins!" He shook his head and laughed at the idea—it was altogether too absurd and incredible.

CHAPTER 14

Nicholas Miller, too, thought it absurd and incredible when they told him the story. "And what's more, it's impossible," he added. "I've never had a brother in . . . where was it you said?"

"Ullsthorp."

"No, definitely not." Nicholas Miller gave them a friendly grin and went back to his work. He was busy filling two big barrels with flour, and the air around him was one big white cloud.

The turning of the wheels and the grinding of the millstones made it difficult to hear much else. Gradually, however, Luke became aware that the miller's son—Viggo, his name was—was shouting and beckoning to him, and Luke followed him out of the mill. "Come on," said Viggo. "Now there are only four to choose among."

Before they could leave, they had to go back into the mill again to fetch Hanna. They almost had to drag her away, for everything in the mill reminded her of Claus

Miller and all her happy memories of those days. But at last they were ready to leave in search of the right Nicholas.

In a town like Ribe there was a great deal to see, especially for Luke and Hanna, who weren't used to towns. For them the ceaseless swarm of people in the streets was something quite new.

Hanna held her nose. "Ugh," she said. "Do all towns smell like this? It was just the same in the one where the flagellants were."

"What does it smell like?" Viggo gave a puzzled laugh; he could smell nothing.

"Nasty, rotten, disgusting. . . . And all the filth you have lying around!"

"I daresay you think it smells better in the villages?"

"Certainly," Hanna answered without hesitation. "There it only smells of animals: horses, cows, pigs—and the dung heap, of course, but then you know what that's like!"

"Of course." Viggo grinned. "If you can't stand town smells, you should live in the country."

Meanwhile, they were making their way along a street, zigzagging to avoid the piebald pigs rooting around in the filth and the cats and dogs that were fighting or relieving themselves all over the refuse.

Suddenly Luke missed his footing and sank up to his knees in something that smelled even worse than the rest. "Ugh," he said, and spat. Then he waded quickly back onto firm ground. "Give me a proper dung heap every time—you know where you are with that. But what the devil is this doing *here?*"

Viggo laughed. "Ah, we have some very particular people around here."

"Particular?" Hanna wrinkled her nose. "You're joking!"

"No!" Viggo chuckled. "They're so particular that they don't go outside to sit like the rest of us. Oh no, they make a little room in a corner of their house and go and sit there!"

"What kind of room is that?"

"It's called the privy," Viggo answered with a laugh. "Privy means secret, but everyone knows what the secret is when they go and empty it into a hole in the street. They're not supposed to, but they do!"

"But what a place to choose to empty it!" Hanna exclaimed. "Here, where everybody has to pass—they must be pigs!"

"People are so lazy," Viggo answered. "They can't be bothered carrying the stuff any farther. And that I can well understand—it smells awful. But I've seen them with my own eyes. They do it early in the morning, before people are up and about. And then they quickly shovel a little dust over it, or a bucket of ashes, so it won't be too obvious. It's a regular man-trap!"

"And you think that's better than a country dung heap!" Hanna retorted.

"Down this way!" Viggo broke in. They had just crossed the river by a narrow wooden bridge. Viggo pointed along the river, where a row of houses stood at a convenient distance from the water.

"What's that?" asked Luke. He had caught sight of something that had made him deaf to Viggo's words and to everything else. He stood stock still pointing at something that lay in the water alongside the road they were following.

"That?" Viggo snorted. "Have you never seen a boat before?"

"A sailing boat," Luke put in hastily. He didn't want the other to think them complete simpletons.

"There aren't many of them here at present," Viggo explained. "You wait till the autumn, though. All the boats are laid up here for the winter—the place is solid with them. Big ships, little boats, rafts, barges, anything you care to mention. They stretch all the way to the castle and beyond."

Luke went to the water's edge, to the structure of stakes and planks that had been built all the way along the river. Boats bobbed up and down, as if nestling against the stakes they were fastened to.

He climbed down a ladder that led into the water and gave his legs a good wash. When he had surfaced again, he began counting the boats. There were six small ones and one that was rather bigger, with a roof over it and a thick pole projecting high into the air.

"What kind of boat is that?" he asked, pointing at it.

"It's a salt boat from Lüneburg," Viggo answered.

Hanna gazed at it in wonder. "Salt boat?" she asked.

"That's right. They sell salt here—and they sail all the way here and back again! Where did you think salt came from?"

Hanna and Luke were at a loss, but Viggo repeated what he had heard so often. "First they sail down a river till they reach the sea, and finally they come here, up the river Ribe."

They had almost forgotten what they were there for. Everything was so new and exciting that they could happily have spent the whole day watching it all, staring at the people in the streets and on the wharfs—so different from the people who lived in the villages.

But Viggo was getting impatient. "Come on," he said.

"It's all very well for him," thought Luke. "He sees it every day."

Viggo led them between two of the mud-built houses. There was just enough room for two people to walk side by side, but the going was made difficult by the doorsteps that kept jutting out and blocking the way.

"They build the houses close together here," said Hanna. "There's hardly room to walk." She stretched out her arms and found she could easily touch the walls of the houses on either side of the narrow alleyway.

"What does that matter?" asked Viggo. "It just makes it easier for the shoemakers to keep each other warm!"

"Shoemakers?"

"Yes, this is the shoemakers' alley. All five of our shoemakers live here. Other people, too," he added. "Here we are, now. This is where Nicholas Shoemaker lives!"

Viggo had stopped at a door, the top half of which stood open. He put his head in and called, "Can we come in, Nicholas Shoemaker?"

"Of course, of course," came a voice from inside. Although Luke was standing right by the door, it was too dark for him to see anyone inside.

Viggo was well known here. He opened the lower half of the door and went in, followed by Hanna and

Luke. As their eyes got used to the half darkness, the shoemaker and his workbench came gradually into view. He was sitting on a three-legged stool, stitching a black boot. When the three children came in, he looked up from his work, first at their faces and then at their bare feet.

"Are your feet cold?" he asked contentedly. "In that case, Nicholas Shoemaker will soon make you some nice warm boots. You've come to the right place; there are boots here at every price."

"No, no," said Viggo hastily, "we don't want boots this side of Michaelmas; we want a couple of words with you."

Luke and Hanna watched the shoemaker anxiously while Viggo—using rather more than a couple of words—explained in great detail about their search for Uncle Nicholas.

The shoemaker was a short, stocky man, a little stiff and angular from sitting in the same position all the time. He was almost completely bald on top, with a streak of greasy gray hair, much the same color as his leather apron, falling over his neck. The room smelled vilely of rancid grease and animal hides.

"No," said the shoemaker when Viggo had finally come to the end of his story. "I'm Ribe born and bred, and I never had a brother, more's the pity! I had no fewer than five sisters—and I often felt the lack of a brother."

"Ah, well," said Viggo, "we must try again. There are still three places left. One of them is bound to be the right one!"

Next on the list was Nicholas Woodcarver, right over by the South Gate. They threaded their way through narrow streets choked with filth, and others that were a little wider and a little cleaner. Again, there was almost too much for Hanna and Luke to see.

Their route took them past the most enormous building they had ever seen. "That's the cathedral," Viggo told them.

It was so high that they had to crane their necks to see the doves sitting up on the green roof, and soaring above the rest of the building, far into the heavens, were the towers. To Hanna it seemed as if they might come crashing down on her at any moment, so she wanted to go another way.

While they stood gazing at the walls, the towers, the doors, and the statues, the world seemed suddenly to be engulfed in one tremendous din. The bells began ringing —first in the cathedral, then in the town's six churches and four monasteries. The voices of the bells had a strangely agitating effect—it was the most awesome thing they had ever experienced—and they put their hands to their ears.

Luke felt how wretchedly small they were—like ants or other insects crawling in the crevices at the foot of these mighty towers. "It . . . it wasn't people," he whispered when the bells had fallen silent and the town's normal hubbub could be heard again. "I mean, people could never have built such . . ."

"They did, you know," said Viggo. "But it took them a long time. A hundred years, probably."

Hanna said nothing. She knew it was impossible for

men to build so high. God himself must have helped them, or at least some of His angels.

When they came to the woodcarver's house, they found the door barred. Viggo, never at a loss, went next door to inquire. He was there for some time.

"The plague . . ." he said on his return. "That Nicholas is dead. His whole family's dead or gone away."

"What if it was him?" said Luke after a pause.

"It wasn't!" Viggo reassured him. "Because they told me he only had three brothers and they all lived in this street. No, it wasn't him!"

Hanna sighed. "Now there are only two left," she thought. "If it isn't one of them, then Luke and I are all alone, and we shall have to go back to Matthew and Marta and the little boys."

Luke was tense. "Where does the next one live?" he asked. In his heart he was afraid they weren't going to succeed—and what then?

"Just around the corner!" Viggo was off already. They turned into a side street and stopped outside a small house.

"Here!" he exclaimed. "This is where the next Nicholas lives. He's the schoolmaster at the cathedral school. I'm sorry for you if it's him—he beats all the boys in the school once a day with the rope or the birch—one or the other. Still, I suppose we'd better ask if it's him."

All this Viggo had managed to get out at breathless speed as they stood on the steps. Then he hammered hard on the knocker.

"Did you say schoolmaster?" Luke whispered. "What does that mean?"

"It means he's in a school," answered Viggo, "a place

where you learn to read and write. And he doesn't half know how to beat boys," he continued in a whisper. "The ones from his school are black and blue on their backsides for days afterwards!"

"Hm," murmured Luke. For the first time he was beginning to hope that the man living behind the door was *not* Uncle Nicholas.

"It's true," said Viggo as if someone had contradicted him. "I've seen it with my own eyes. They're striped all over most of the time until they get themselves a pair of really good leather trousers—to wear under their ordinary trousers. Otherwise, they'd be made to take their trousers down—and that's not so funny, except for the others sitting there laughing their heads off."

"Can't we . . . can't we skip this one and try the last Nicholas?" whispered Hanna, but by now it was too late.

The door opened. A tall, heavily built man in a long black gown came out. He had a goose quill in one hand and inkstains on his powerful fingers.

"What do you want?" he asked. His great beard, black with streaks of gray, reached to his chest and trembled as he spoke.

Before they could answer, he went on, "I can't take any more in my school this year. There's only Master Gotius and myself left—of the schoolmasters who are any good! There are a couple of young whippersnappers, of course, but . . . no, we can't take any more this year. Perhaps next year—provided we get proper teachers." He was about to shut the door when he remembered something important. "I suppose you can pay?"

"We . . . we don't want to go to school," Viggo

stammered. He was quite nervous; it wasn't every day of the week that you stood face to face with such a mighty man, who not only kept a school, but also kept people's children striped at one end all the year around. "We only wanted to ask if—if you had a brother." That was as much as he could get out.

"A brother?" Schoolmaster Nicholas looked bewildered. He stood there rubbing his nose with an inky finger, and the big red nose began to change color.

Luke pulled himself together and explained that he was looking for his Uncle Nicholas.

For a moment, as the schoolmaster stood there listening, he looked quite human. But as soon as he understood he shook his head grimly and said, "No, indeed. My brothers are all either schoolmasters or priests. There are no dirty peasants in our family! I'm busy," he concluded, and he strode back into his house and slammed the door.

Viggo was quite red in the face, and Luke heaved a sigh of relief. "That was a stroke of luck," he said quietly. "Where does the fifth one live?"

"He lives outside the town, to the west—out at Ribe Castle. He's a watchman."

"Watchman?"

"A man who keeps watch at the city gate, or up on the tower."

"If only it's him," said Luke, wondering what they should do if it wasn't. Should they go to Master Martin and Birgitta?

Never had they seen anything like Ribe Castle. It stood perched on a hill and could be reached only by crossing a ditch filled with water, which surrounded it on every side. They walked around the ditch, looking at the castle from several sides. There was only one place to cross the ditch, by means of a plank bridge, and enter the castle.

"Who lives there?" Hanna asked warily. She hardly dared to speak because of all the people standing or walking in the road. Most of them looked busy.

"Kings!" said Viggo, who was proud of his town.

"Is the king living there now?" Luke was curious to know. He knew that a king was a mighty man who ruled the land, but people seldom thought or talked about him where Luke lived.

"No, not now. But several kings have lived here."

For a time they stood gazing at the great castle, with its green roof and glass windows. There were even windows one above the other in several "stories," as Viggo pointed out to make them understand that he knew what was what.

"And where does Nicholas Watchman live?" Luke asked suddenly. He could not keep his thoughts off the all-absorbing topic.

"There!" Viggo pointed. A short distance from the moat stood a little group of houses. "That's where the tower watchmen and gate watchmen live—and the others who protect our town. There he comes—that's him—I'm almost certain!"

A tall man in a bright blue and red uniform was coming toward them along the road from the direction of the houses.

Luke caught a glimpse of a long, shiny object dangling from his shoulder. "What's that?" he asked. "That bright thing?"

"It's his horn! When he blows that, you can hear it all over the town—and then all the men come running because they know there's something wrong."

Meanwhile, Nicholas Watchman was coming nearer.

"Do you really dare to talk to him?" whispered Hanna. She had been struck almost dumb by everything she had seen—but she would probably talk all the more when the excitement was over.

"Yes, of course," muttered Viggo.

There was no need to do anything to stop the watchman. When he reached the boys, he stopped of his own accord. "Hello," he said. "What's going on here?"

"Good afternoon, Nicholas Watchman!" said Viggo, bowing politely—not because this was his normal behavior, but because he knew the watchman attached great importance to that kind of thing. "We've come here to talk to you."

"To me?" The watchman looked astonished. "What can you have to talk to me about?"

Viggo hastened to explain—you never knew when a man like that might decide it was time for him to be moving on.

The watchman crossed himself when he heard about the plague taking everyone in the village except for Luke. Then he shook his head. "No, I only had two brothers, and they both died many years ago."

Luke's head began to spin. "But aren't there any more Nicholases in Ribe?" he asked.

"Why, yes." The watchman started counting on his

fingers. "There's . . . let me see . . . there's five of us—no, four since the plague."

"And we've asked them all!"

"That's unfortunate for you, isn't it?"

They returned to the mill without another word.

CHAPTER 15

There were so many people in this town that they overflowed onto every street, talking, shouting, laughing, scolding, or even being quiet. Every single one was called something—Simon, Olaf, Michael, Niels, Hans—but not one of them was called Nicholas except, of course, for the four they had met: the miller, the shoemaker, the schoolmaster, and the watchman. The right Nicholas was not to be found, but they were still searching.

"We just have to keep going," thought Luke. "Keep going and keep going, like the bees. Street by street, one man after another, one woman after another, one boy or girl after another."

It was always the same: "That's right, there's Nicholas Schoolmaster, Nicholas Miller, and . . . and . . ."

Yes, yes, of course. But never anything new. No more Nicholases!

It was difficult to keep going, to plod endlessly around the streets asking, "Do you know anybody called Nicholas?" And they could not stay with the miller's wife. To sleep in the mill at night was as much as they were allowed. It was cold there, and every morning they were white from sleeping among the barrels and sacks of flour.

The miller's wife was a shrew, as they knew from eating at her table once in a while. Her tongue was in constant motion, like a grindstone. It hardly even stopped wagging while she was eating. All day long she was talking, usually scolding. Viggo even declared that she could talk while she was asleep—but he was probably only boasting.

No, they couldn't stay there; they must find another place.

"It's hopeless. Quite hopeless!" They had sat down for a rest on a step somewhere in the town. It was exhausting to walk around all day long in a town like this, and Hanna and Luke were tired, footsore, and gray with dust. Viggo had long since given up. He had lost all inclination for the search and was much more interested in learning to sail the raft.

Hanna sighed. "Yes, it's hopeless. And so . . . ?"

"So it's hopeless, that's all!"

"Yes, but what are we going to do?" Hanna was not content to leave it at that.

"We must go," mumbled Luke. He was sitting with his chin in his hands, his elbows on his knees, and his feet on the stone step.

"Yes, but where?"

"We must just go," said Luke. "It's no good asking me where. You're a Sunday's child, and if you don't know who can? Shall we go back to Master Martin and Birgitta and her kind mother? They were all so nice and friendly, and they said we could come—both of us."

Hanna shook her head. "I'd rather go to Matthew

and Marta and the two little boys—I don't know the others!"

"It will be a long walk. Do you think we shall find them?"

Hanna nodded. "With the help of the saints!"

They sat for a long time in silence. There was no shortage of places where they could stay. All the empty houses and farms with black crosses tarred on the walls were simply standing and waiting for people.

Hanna said, "Do you think there is anyone . . . at home?"

Luke needed to think about that. He wrinkled his brow. "Where do you mean 'home'?"

"In Finthorp!"

"I don't know about that," answered Luke. "But I'd give anything to see Ullsthorp at this moment! Just to see it again. Though of course there are no people there any more!"

The conversation petered out. They both knew that they must set out on their travels again; there was no alternative. But neither of them knew where they should go.

Across the street a gate opened. Hanna and Luke looked in the direction of the gate, which was set in a high wall. A man came into view—a man such as they had seldom seen on their journey—a monk in a gray robe, a Franciscan friar.

After shutting the gate, he stood for a moment, adjusting his cowl over his head. He was evidently a young man: his movements were youthful, his walk was youthful, and when he came nearer, they could see that his eyes, too, were youthful. "God's peace!" He had stopped directly in front of them.

"Amen!" they responded. They knew there were many monks and friars in Ribe because there were as many as four monasteries. Even if the plague had hit them severely, they were still a common sight in the streets, but this was the first time they had talked to one.

The Franciscan looked at them with his mild eyes and said, "Why are you sitting on these steps?"

"We don't know," said Luke. He was still sitting with his chin resting on his hands. "There are only four Nicholases in the whole of Ribe—and that's too few. We need a fifth!"

He was talking mainly to himself, as he had done so often of late, but the Franciscan listened attentively. "Tell me the whole story," he said. "You're a whole person, so you mustn't only tell half a story."

Luke looked up at the friar, and although he was sick and tired of the whole subject, he told him about the plague, the deserted villages, and their search for Uncle Nicholas. The Franciscan listened carefully and gave an encouraging nod whenever Luke showed signs of stopping.

Hanna sat in silence, looking at the friar. It was the first time she had seen one so close. "He's feeling sorry for Luke and me," she thought. "He would gladly help us if he could. Now he's wondering what he can do."

When Luke had finished speaking, Hanna said, "I'm sure you can help us!"

The friar smiled, though he seemed a little taken aback.

"And you're the only person who can," Hanna continued.

"What makes you think that?"

She became a little confused. A moment ago it had been quite clear in her mind that the friar was the one man who could help them.

"I . . . I could see from your face . . . just now," she stammered. "You've heard the name Nicholas, Nicholas from Ullsthorp?"

The Franciscan gave a rapid little shake of the head. It was not clear whether he was saying no or shaking some thought away. Whichever it was, he stood for a long time without moving or saying anything. He seemed to be deep in thought over something. His eyes never saw them. "Come with me," he said suddenly. "I want to help you if I can."

They followed him through the gate into the monastery garden. "I don't really know if I can help you," he said, "but I can find out. I've got an idea! Wait here till I return."

The Franciscan went, and the two children were left on their own in the monastery garden. They had never been in such a place before. It was full of flowers and herbs, and the scent was so strong as to make them feel almost faint.

"Do you really think he can help us?" Hanna whispered. She was hardly aware that she was whispering; perhaps it was because she knew it was a house of God, or perhaps because it was so big, or even perhaps because their search seemed to be over.

Luke simply shook his head. He had been disappointed so often in the last few days, and now he kept wondering where they should go next. They had to leave Ribe—perhaps the very next day. The Franciscan was their last hope.

They were so wrapped in their gloomy thoughts that they failed to notice a man coming to join them in the garden. Suddenly, there he stood—another Franciscan. His cowl was pulled back, revealing a wreath of brown hair around his bald crown. "God's peace!" he said.

"Amen," answered Hanna, looking closely at the friar. Was he the one who was going to help them? Luke, too, looked at him, and something seemed to stir in his mind, only he could not quite make out what it was.

"Brother John told me you were here," said the friar.

"There's something about his voice," thought Luke.

"Will you tell me in your own words why you've come here?" the Franciscan continued. "Brother John may have left something out."

Luke began his story, but forgot half of it, and Hanna had to help him out several times.

"What is it about him?" thought Luke.

The Franciscan kept his eyes on Luke throughout the tale until the boy ended by saying they needed a fifth Nicholas.

The Franciscan cleared his throat. "What's your name?" he asked.

"Luke. Luke Janson from Ullsthorp." The friar gave a little start. He gazed at Luke for a long time.

"You're like your father!" he said at last. "Jan looked just like you at your age!"

"What, you mean"—Hanna gasped for breath—"you mean you're really . . . so you're Uncle Nicholas!"

The Franciscan smiled. "Yes, I'm Jan's brother

Nicholas!" Then he looked at Hanna. "And what's your name?" he asked. "Are you another of Jan's sons?"

Hanna shook her head vigorously. "No, I'm a girl. My name is Hanna."

The friar looked at her a little more closely. "So you're Jan's daughter?"

"No!" she shook her head again. "I'm just Claus Miller's little girl from Finthorp! But . . . but I do belong to the family because Grandma Miller always said . . ." Hanna was quite carried away, and she grew red in the face. "No," she said, "but we've been together so long—and been separated so long—and now we want always to be together!"

Luke stood and stared at his new uncle. The one possibility that had never occurred to him was that he might be a monk or a friar. It came as a great surprise. "I never thought you could be a monk," he said at last. "Never!" He shook his head in wonder. "Mother said to me that time just before she died: 'Go to your Uncle Nicholas at Ribe. He's a good man, and the only man you can turn to. He's your father's brother, and after God he's your next best hope, if he's still alive.' But she never said you were a monk. I never thought. I thought you were an ordinary peasant."

Brother Nicholas smiled. "Your mother didn't know either because I wasn't a monk when I said good-bye to them at home in Ullsthorp." He sighed and seemed far away in his thoughts. Then he became aware of them again and asked, "What do you intend to do now?"

The children looked at each other. Until that moment they had thought only of going to Ribe and finding Uncle Nicholas. Never once had they thought what they would do after that. They had taken it for granted that Uncle Nicholas would solve the problem for them.

Luke cleared his throat. "I . . . I don't know!" He could hear how silly this sounded, so he added hurriedly, "But . . . but now we have you!"

Brother Nicholas smiled again; then he looked thoughtful. He had suddenly become responsible for two small human beings, and he had hardly had time to think about the problem.

"Would you like to stay in the monastery?"

He didn't mean it seriously, but he felt he had to say something—and the question popped out of him.

For what seemed to Hanna a long time, the question remained unanswered. "No," she said at last. She spoke quietly, but her mind was made up.

"No," she repeated a little louder. "We don't want to live in a monastery. We want to live out in the country on a farm." She was a little surprised herself at what she was saying, but she felt there was no choice. It had to be said.

"That's right," Luke mumbled.

Brother Nicholas looked at Hanna in some surprise. He had lived in the monastery for so many years that he had forgotten what a fourteen-year-old girl is like.

"You see, we want to stay together," she added. "Why don't the others say anything?" she thought. Then she continued herself: "Grandma Miller said our village would be emptied of people—and it was. She also said that I would meet a boy my own age—and that we would set out on a long and difficult journey."

Hanna paused for breath. "Luke and I are nearly the same age. I was fourteen on Saint Anne's day, and he will be soon on Saint Nicholas's day. We have had a long and very difficult journey. It must certainly be him that Grandma Miller meant. She also said that I should bake his bread, bear his children, and tend his hearth, until I was as old as she was, until I, too, was a grandmother and . . ."

Hanna came to a stop. She had become so excited that she was almost unaware of her words. Her cheeks burned and her heart beat violently. For the first time since Luke had been with Hanna, he was at a loss what to say. The whole thing was beyond his comprehension.

Brother Nicholas looked at the two young people who had wandered through the plague-stricken land. They had come all that distance specially to find him! He wondered how he could best help them? He was accustomed to the peaceful life of a monastery, and he was bound by his vow of service to God in the monastery—in the monastery? An old thought suddenly came back to him—the thought that he might serve God another way.

Suddenly there they stood, these children brimming over with life! They had the courage to live, even if their entire families had been wiped out and their villages laid waste! All at once he could see them clearly, wandering through the dead, desolate land.

They were two ordinary human children, and yet they were the kind who helped the country through difficult times—through war and plague, pestilence and famine. The pious monk felt for a moment that he must bow down before them, before the life in them, before their will to go on living.

"Yes," he said at last. "You *shall* live out in the country. You are needed there—for your work and for your lives!" Then he gave a deep sigh. "I must go and talk with Abbot Peter," he said. "Come with me to the brother who keeps the gate. He will show you where you can spend the evening, or the night, if I don't come back before then!"

Before leaving them Brother Nicholas added, "Because there's something very serious I have to say to Abbot Peter."

It was morning two days later. Out through the north gate of Ribe came three people: a Franciscan friar, a girl, and a boy.

The Franciscan had gathered up his long robe and fastened it securely in his belt, revealing his strong, bare legs. In his hand he carried a long staff. At his back dangled a large leather bag, which he heaved up until it was lying comfortably on his broad shoulders.

Each of the two children also had a bag on their shoulders. The girl was holding her nose as she walked. She said nothing, but the boy noticed what she was doing. He knew that she was not yet accustomed to the smells of Ribe.

"Take good note of that smell," he said teasingly. "It's the last chance you'll get."

"Thank goodness," said the girl.

They proceeded briskly on their way. Soon they had reached the last landmark in the town—the gallows hill! At present the place was not too forbidding. The gallows and the hovering ravens were out of business. The plague had done their job, for a long time to come!

"It's strange," said Luke. "I never thought we'd be going back again."

Brother Nicholas smiled. "Abbot Peter understood me in the end, even if it took him half the night. There's so much to do. That's why we can't all stay in the monastery. Some of us must go out into the world. We must go out and serve as priests for all the people living out here in the countryside."

"What exactly did you say to him—the Abbot?" Hanna made no attempt to hide her curiosity. She knew soon after she met him that she liked Uncle Nicholas, that she need not be afraid of asking him anything!

"Yes, what did I say?" Nicholas knit his eyebrows. "I wonder if I can remember."

"That voice!" Luke thought once again. "It's my father he reminds me of."

"Ah, yes," said Brother Nicholas. "I think I must have said something about there being many villages without a priest, like sheep without a shepherd."

"That's very true," said Luke. "Martin the bell ringer and Dorothea needed a priest so that they could get married properly!"

They walked on a little in silence, each thinking his own thoughts. The landscape here was flat. It was full of weeds, great docks and thistles, with scattered trees and hawthorns. One or two cart tracks wound their way north.

"Is it really true?" asked Hanna. "Are we going home —to Finthorp?" She was asking herself almost as much as the others. It was so good to talk about it.

"Yes," said Brother Nicholas. "We'll go first to your village, then on to Ullsthorp."

Luke hardly knew how to express the difficult

thought that had occurred to him. "What if there are still no people there—neither in Hanna's village nor in mine. What then?"

"There are still plenty of places for us," Brother Nicholas answered with a smile. "We'll go to some other place where they need us."

Again they walked on in silence until Hanna said, "Somewhere where they need a priest?"

"Yes!"

"And where there's a farm for us?"

Luke had started to think seriously about the work. "A farm with cows, calves, pigs, hens, and so on?"

"Yes—a good, solid farm," said Nicholas.

"Can we live with you?" Luke asked. "In the priest's house?"

Hanna giggled. "With Master Nicholas."

Uncle Nicholas laughed. "Or the priest could live in a farmhouse."

"That would be nice!" Hanna danced for joy.

"But," Nicholas said, raising his forefinger, "it's only to begin with that you're going to live with me. Later you must manage for yourselves, and then perhaps it will be for me to live with you."

Hanna became still more enthusiastic. "You'll be very welcome," she said, "even if Grandma Miller never said anything about a priest sharing my hearth!"

"Ah, but the priest belongs to the family," Nicholas said with a laugh. "I expect that's why she didn't think she need mention it."

Hanna, too, began laughing, and she in turn infected Luke. All three laughed as they walked. The laughter welled up from deep down inside them and washed away all the dark memories. Life was good after all. It was stronger than plague or death.

A flock of ravens flew up in alarm from a tree bordering the road. For a moment their hoarse cries spoiled the beauty of the day, but soon they vanished southward.

The three continued on their way, their figures growing smaller and smaller. Soon they would disappear from sight among the hawthorns and thistles, but for the moment they could still be seen and heard from the town. And they were still laughing!